DOUBLE THE BOUNTY

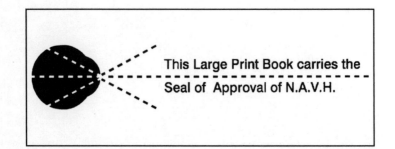

This Large Print Book carries the
Seal of Approval of N.A.V.H.

DOUBLE THE BOUNTY

ROBERT J. RANDISI

WHEELER PUBLISHING
A part of Gale, Cengage Learning

GALE
CENGAGE Learning

Detroit • New York • San Francisco • New Haven, Conn • Waterville, Maine • London

GALE
CENGAGE Learning™

Copyright © 1987 by Robert Randisi.
Wheeler Publishing, a part of Gale, Cengage Learning.

Wheeler Publishing Large Print Western.
The text of this Large Print edition is unabridged.
Other aspects of the book may vary from the original edition.
Set in 16 pt. Plantin.

LIBRARY OF CONGRESS CATALOGING-IN-PUBLICATION DATA

Randisi, Robert J.
    Double the bounty / by Robert J. Randisi. — Large print ed.
        p. cm. — (Wheeler Publishing large print western)
    ISBN-13: 978-1-4104-2935-3 (pbk.)
    ISBN-10: 1-4104-2935-0 (pbk.)
    1. Bounty hunters—Fiction. 2. Large type books. I. Title.
PS3568.A53D68 2010
813'.54—dc21   2010016380

Published in 2010 by arrangement with Dominick Abel Literary Agency, Inc.

Printed in the United States of America
1 2 3 4 5 6 7 14 13 12 11 10

DOUBLE THE BOUNTY

PROLOGUE

HEARTLESS, WYOMING

Brian Foxx knew he was a legend.

Oh, maybe he wasn't as much of a legend as he wanted to be — but then no man ever is — except for Wild Bill Hickok. Hickok was the only man in history who might have been more famous than even he believed.

And Brian Foxx was certainly no Wild Bill Hickok.

Brian Foxx was a bank and train robber, and he was wanted in three states for robberies committed over the past two years. What made Brian Foxx a legend was the fact that he had robbed two banks on the same day on more than one occasion — hundreds of miles apart! It was physically impossible, yet witnesses in both places had identified the man as Brian Foxx, whose face had adorned enough posters and newspapers to be recognized.

Brian Foxx sat in a straight-backed wooden chair across the street from the Bank of Heartless, Wyoming. He was observing the bank's activities, as he always did before robbing one. Also, he knew that he still had two days before everything would be set for the robbery to take place.

He had to wait for his twin brother, Brent Foxx, to get into position hundreds of miles away in Doverville, Arizona. This way they could rob their respective banks at the same time.

Witnesses would *swear* that the man who robbed the bank was the infamous Brian Foxx.

This would certainly add to his legend!

II
DENVER, COLORADO

In Denver, Colorado, inside the federal marshal's office, Marshal Charles Edward Chesbro counted out one thousand dollars into the hand of a tall, dark-haired man with dark, penetrating eyes and a heavy mustache.

"Cole was a little worse for wear when you brought him in here yesterday," the marshal said after he'd finished his counting.

"He was alive, wasn't he?" the other man

8

asked. He counted the money himself, which seemed to annoy the marshal.

"Uh, what are you going to do with all that money?"

The man put the money away and looked at the marshal.

"That's none of your damned business. You got any new paper?"

"Outside on the wall," the marshal said, stung by the reproach.

Without a word of thanks or good-bye, the man turned and walked outside.

The marshal shook his head, watching the man's retreating back. He couldn't understand why the man's presence — no matter how many times he had dragged a prisoner back here — always unnerved him.

Outside, the man looked over the posters. He stopped at the one that said:

WANTED: BRIAN FOXX
$1500 REWARD
DEAD OR ALIVE

The man took the bottom of the poster between his thumb and forefinger and snapped it off the wall.

Poster in hand, he walked to his horse, a small but powerfully built gelding, and mounted up. Hanging from his saddle pommel, in plain sight, was an expertly tied hangman's noose.

The man's name was Decker. And he was something of a legend himself.

He was a bounty hunter.

■ ■ ■ ■

PART ONE:
FOXX HOLE

■ ■ ■ ■

CHAPTER I

Decker directed John Henry, his nine-year-old gelding, down the main street of Heartless, Wyoming. Somebody was in a piss-poor mood when they named this town, Decker thought.

Decker commanded attention as he rode down the street. His tall, muscular frame sat straight in the saddle beneath a flat-brimmed black hat, and he rode with an air of confidence that women found arresting and men, threatening. Men found the dark eyes penetrating, as if Decker was able to look inside of them and discover their deepest secrets.

Women, on the other hand, found his eyes expressive. He looked as if he was concerned with how he could please them the most. Most women enjoyed the feeling it gave them in the pit of their stomachs.

Of course, the fact that Decker looked at all men with suspicion, and upon all women with respect, may have had something to do with it. Women sensed the respect he had for them, and appreciated it. Men feared he would see them for what they were, while women feared he would not see them at all.

And then there was that hangman's noose, which quickly identified him to one and all. And if that wasn't enough, there was the weapon he wore on his hip. It was a shotgun that had been sawed off at both the barrels and the stock and then slipped into a specially made holster. The whole rig had been designed for him by a gunsmith friend when Decker discovered that he was almost hopeless with a handgun. With the shotgun he rarely had to aim to hit his target, and with a rifle he was . . . adequate.

With a rope, however, he was deadly.

Decker rode up to the Bank of Heartless and halted. He didn't dismount but simply gazed at the bank, taking in every aspect of the structure. This was one of the two banks that Brian Foxx was supposed to have robbed. Foxx could not have been in both banks at one time, but Decker had to start somewhere, and he chose Wyoming over Arizona, since Denver, where he had picked up the poster, was closer to Wyoming.

He asked ol' John Henry to walk again, promising him that it would only be as far as the livery stable.

"After that you get a well-deserved rest, you old scudder."

John Henry shook his head in reply and started walking. Decker claimed no friends, unless a man could be friends with a horse.

When he reached the livery, he dismounted and was met by the liveryman, a grizzled old soul who looked close to seventy.

"Old horse," the man said, accepting the reins.

"This horse will run anything you have in your livery into the ground."

The man cast a critical eye over John Henry's lines, spat a gob of tobacco juice, and said, "Don't doubt it."

"Treat him good and maybe he won't bite your hand off." Decker tossed the man fifty cents.

"I always treat them right," he said, waggling both hands at Decker and adding, "that's why I still got all my fingers after thirty years of handling horses."

"Then I've got nothing to worry about, do I?"

The old-timer spat another gob of tobacco juice at some unseen target and said, "Nope."

Decker took his saddlebags and rifle from

his saddle and was about to leave when the old man said, "What about this thing?"

Decker turned and saw the old man pointing to the hangman's noose.

"Just leave it where it is," Decker replied. "It's not hurting anybody."

Decker set off in the direction of the hotel. First stop was the saloon for a drink, and then the sheriff's office for a talk.

The saloon was called the Oak Tree Saloon. Over a cold beer he questioned the bartender about the name.

"Well," the man said, rubbing the lower portion of his florid face with a thick-fingered hand, "when they started to build this here town, there was this big oak tree standing right on this spot. Well, they cleared all the land around here, but that dang oak just didn't want to budge. They finally decided to use dynamite, but some dang fool used too much." He pointed over to the wall over the bar where a long oak branch was hanging and said, "That's all that was left of that stubborn old oak."

Decker doubted the validity of the story, but had to admit that it sounded good.

"Who's the sheriff of this town?" he asked.

"That'd be Hack Wilson."

Decker put his beer down.

"Thomas 'Hack' Wilson?"

"That's right. You know him?"

"I know him. How long has he been sheriff here?"

" 'Bout eight months or so."

Eight months. Well, maybe the people of this town had already caught on to old Hack's ways and were ready to vote him out come next election. It wasn't any of Decker's business. He was only concerned with the Brian Foxx bank robbery. All he wanted was to talk to Hack Wilson.

"Thanks for the beer."

"Stayin' in town?"

"Might be."

"If you are, come on back for another. I got another story for you if you didn't like that one."

"I liked it fine," Decker said. "If I'm staying, I'll be back."

He walked from the saloon directly to the sheriff's office. A wooden sign saying, THOMAS WILSON, TOWN SHERIFF, hung outside. He rapped his knuckles on the door a few times and entered.

"Sheriff," he said.

Sheriff Wilson's head was bowed over his desk as he perused some paperwork, and when he looked up Decker saw that it was indeed Hack Wilson.

And Wilson recognized Decker.

"Decker!"

"Hello, Sheriff."

"What can I do for you, Decker," Wilson asked nervously. "Hunting somebody?"

"That's what I'm doing, all right." When Decker dropped his saddlebags onto the back of a straight-backed wooden chair, Wilson jumped at the sound, looking nervous again.

"Relax, Wilson," Decker said, "I ain't gonna bite *you*."

It had been three years ago when Wilson had decided to try his hand at bounty hunting. They had a disagreement over a prisoner and Wilson — a large man even then — decided he wanted to fight about it. Well, after a few minutes he realized he'd made a mistake. His bulk worked against him while Decker, whipcord thin and fast, had given Wilson a lesson in hand to hand. That was before Wilson decided to use his teeth. He sank his teeth into Decker's arm, making Decker angry — he'd been only mildly annoyed until that point. Decker knocked Wilson cold. After that, he'd had to go to a doctor to have the human bite disinfected. Upon returning to the scene of the battle, he found Wilson and the prisoner gone!

"Now, that was three years ago, Decker —" Wilson began nervously.

"You remember, eh?"

"I been sorry as hell about that ever since, but I needed the money."

"Nobody needs money that bad, Wilson. Do the people of this town know what kind of a thieving buzzard they've got for a sheriff?"

"I been a good sheriff here, Decker. I — I'm trying to do right for a change."

"Is that so?"

"And I'll prove it to you. Just tell me what you want and it's yours."

"All right," Decker said, deciding to take the man up on his offer. "Brian Foxx."

Wilson was taken aback, then realized that it made perfect sense.

"I should have known you'd get on his trail sooner or later. There ain't much I can tell you. I got to the bank after it was all over. I never saw the man."

"You can tell me who did."

"Sure, I can do that. In fact, I'd be glad to take you around to the witnesses myself." Wilson rose from behind his desk to do just that. In his midthirties, he had let his gut grow to alarming proportions.

"We can go in a little while," Decker said. "I'd like to get a hotel room first, freshen up, and get something to eat. Two hours all right with you?"

"Sure, Decker, fine," Wilson said.

"All right." Decker picked up his saddle-bags and said, "Two hours, then."

"I'll be here."

Decker pinned the man with a hard stare. "I know you will."

CHAPTER II

Decker, refreshed and fed, stopped off at the telegraph office before going to the saloon for a beer. He composed a short telegram to the sheriff of Doverville, Arizona, asking for a complete and detailed description of the man who had held up their bank the month before. He also asked for a quick reply. He paid for the telegram and told the clerk he'd check in for an answer later.

When he entered the saloon, the bartender recognized him.

"Another beer?"

"Yep."

"And another story?"

"Just the beer. I'll make do with the first story."

"Coming up."

When the bartender came back with the beer, Decker said, "Tell me about the sheriff."

"What about him?"

"What kind of a lawman is he?"

The man shrugged.

"Fair to middlin', I guess. He keeps the peace, stops in for a free drink every once in a while."

"He looks like he's getting a lot of free meals."

"Might be, but he was shaped like that when he ran for the office."

Decker noticed something odd in the bartender's voice and mentioned it.

"Well, to tell you the God's honest truth, Mr. . . ."

"Decker."

"Name's Ted Daniels," the bartender said, and they shook hands. "To tell you the truth, Decker, Hack Wilson ran unopposed for the office because nobody else wanted the job."

"Why's that?"

"Would you like to be the sheriff of a town called Heartless?"

"That's another thing. Why is the town called Heartless?"

The bartender leaned on his elbows and said, "Somebody was in a piss-poor mood when they named it."

Wilson was waiting at his office when

Decker arrived.

"Ready?" Decker asked.

"I'm ready."

They left the office and Wilson dictated the direction they would take.

"How many people were in the bank that day?"

"Four. The manager, the teller, and two customers."

"Let's do the customers first. We can find the other two at the bank."

"It closes at five."

"We've got an hour. I just have a few questions."

The first witness was Thaddeus Bidwell, who ran and owned the hardware store. He replied willingly enough to Decker's questions. He said that he wasn't particularly familiar with Brian Foxx's face, but that the man in the bank had red hair and freckles and had made absolutely no attempt to cover his face.

"Crazy, huh?" the hardware man said.

"Not so crazy, when you consider his motive," Decker replied.

"Which was?"

"He wanted to make sure he got the credit."

■ ■ ■ ■

The second witness was a young woman who was a waitress in the hotel dining room. In fact, it was the waitress who had waited on Decker earlier.

She had been in the bank to make a deposit.

"A small deposit, mind you," she said, smiling crookedly. "On my salary, that's the only kind I can make."

She was a pretty little thing with brown hair and eyes. Probably had suitors up the ass, Decker thought — a pretty ass it was, too.

She described the man exactly as Bidwell had, and added that she knew it was Brian Foxx as soon as she saw him.

"How did you know that?"

"I read the papers, Mr. Decker. I'm not just another pretty face, you know."

"Pretty enough, though, miss," Decker said, tipping his hat. "Darned pretty enough."

"Why, thank you, Mr. Decker."

"And you're a good waitress, too."

"Tell my boss."

"I will. Thank you, miss . . ."

"Benbow, Julia Benbow."

"Miss Benbow."

As Decker and the sheriff left, Julia Benbow experienced a breathless feeling and a tingling in the pit of her stomach.

In the bank Decker asked the same questions of Wilbur Posten, the young teller, and Andrew Billingsworth, the bank manager. Both men described Brian Foxx. Posten added that he had recognized him right away.

"I read the papers," the young man said.

"Do you know Miss Benbow at the hotel?" Decker asked.

The man blushed and said, "I, ah, may have met her." He had obviously met her, since she had an account in this bank, and he had just as obviously noticed her.

"You should go and talk to her. You and she have a lot in common."

"Really?" the man asked, brightening.

"Yeah. She reads the papers, too. Thank you for your time, gentlemen."

"Anything else I can do for you?" Wilson asked, outside the bank.

There was, but Decker didn't want to tell him. He shook his head no and walked away.

He stopped at the telegraph office and found that a reply had come in. He read the message, and it told him just what the four witnesses here had told him.

The bank had been held up by a man in his twenties, with red hair and freckles, who made no attempt to hide his face from three witnesses.

By all accounts, Brian Foxx.

Impossible.

There was only one difference between the two jobs. Here in Heartless, no one had been hurt. In Doverville, a man had been shot and killed.

Brian Foxx was now wanted for murder, as well as bank robbery and train robbery.

That meant an increase in the reward.

Chapter III

The town of Fenner's Fork, in the Utah region, was small and sparsely populated. It did, however, have a saloon and two whores, which made it a perfect place for the Foxx boys, Brian and Brent, to hole up between jobs.

Brian, however, had no intention of allowing either one of them to be caught.

Brian was not only the smartest, he also kept a level head. No one had ever been injured during one of his jobs.

Brent, on the other hand, rarely pulled a job without hurting someone, and Brian usually resigned himself to that fact — but this time Brent had gone too far.

Brian was the first to arrive at Fenner's Fork, and while he waited for Brent, he wondered if — with this recent turn of events — they shouldn't change their area of operation. So far their jobs had been pulled in Wyoming, Arizona, and New

Mexico. Never in Utah, since this was where they rested in between and made their plans.

Maybe, Brian thought, it was time to move things farther west. Maybe try Nevada, Idaho, and Oregon, or even California. On the other hand, they could go east — Kansas, the Indian Territory, and Texas, even to Missouri and Arkansas. If they did that, they could hang their hats in Louisiana. He had always wanted to see New Orleans!

When Brent arrived, he'd have to broach the subject gently in order to get him to agree. His brother had changed since they began this charade. Brent liked the feeling of power and Brian knew that his brother's violent acts were an extension of that. Now that he had actually *killed* someone, what would he be like? And how long would it be before he killed again?

Brian shuddered to think.

Sometimes his brother scared him.

It was a good thing Brent didn't know that, because Brent was intimidated by Brian's superior intelligence, and usually bowed to it. If he ever sensed that Brian was *afraid* of him . . .

He ordered another beer and wondered if he should continue to wait in the saloon or go over and wait with the girls.

CHAPTER IV

When Decker got to the newspaper office, it was almost six and they were getting ready to close up.

"Excuse me?"

There were two people in the place, an old man and a young girl with pigtails. She was very cute and looked to be about fourteen.

"Gettin' ready to close," the old man snapped.

"Oh, Grandpa, don't be so grumpy," the girl said. She walked up to Decker with a big smile on her face. "My name is Felicia Wheeler, what's yours?"

"Decker."

"Pleased to meet you, Mr. Decker. That there's my grandpa, Harrison Wheeler, but everybody just calls him Harry. He's the editor of this newspaper."

"Then he's the man I want to see."

"Well now, like Grandpa said, we're just

getting ready to close."

"I would just like to take a look at some back issues of your paper."

"Oh, then you don't want to talk to the editor," Felicia Wheeler said, "you want to talk to the staff."

"The staff? And who might they be?"

"Me," she said proudly. "I'm them."

Her grandfather came up behind her and said, "Felicia, you gonna be jawing with this stranger all day?"

"Just a little while, Grandpa."

"Well, don't forget to lock up when you leave." The man's hair was as white as snow, and his skin was pink and shiny. His eyes were a crystal-clear blue, and he turned them on Decker now. "This here's my only granddaughter and she's fourteen years old. If you do anything to her besides talk, I'll have to kill you. You understand that?"

"I'll remember, Harry."

The threat was ludicrous, since Harry Wheeler was at least sixty, only about five foot four, and frail, but the sentiment was clear.

"All right."

"See you later, Grandpa," Felicia said.

"Will you be home in time to cook supper, or should I go out?"

"I'll cook, Grandpa. I always cook."

30

The old man left, muttering something that Decker could not catch.

"What back issue you want to see, Mr. Decker?"

"Just call me Decker."

"Fine, and you can call me Felicia."

"I'd like to see whatever issue has stories about Brian Foxx."

"The robber?" she asked, eyes widening. "Are you a lawman?"

"No, I'm not."

She studied him for a moment and then said, "A bounty hunter."

"What makes you say that?"

"You're mean-looking enough for it. What kind of a gun is that for a bounty hunter to carry?"

He looked down at the sawed-off in its special holster and said, "That's so I can be fairly sure I'll hit what I'm aiming at."

"Can't you do that with a forty-five?"

"Never could get the hang of firing a pistol. A rifle's more my weapon. Can I see those papers? Do you have back issues?"

"Oh, sure, in the back room. Come on, I'll get them out for you."

He followed her into the back room, which was filled with stacks of newspapers.

"This looks like a real firetrap," he said. "One match in here . . ."

"All newspaper offices are firetraps, Decker. You just got to be careful." She was looking through stacks of papers and turned to give him a stern look. "You don't smoke, do you?"

"I've been known to on occasion, but I don't have anything with me."

"Well, that's good."

She started to lift a pile of newspapers, and Decker rushed forward to do it for her.

"Just put it on the floor for now. Here's an issue that will interest you. It's dated three months ago, when he held up that bank in Bekins, Wyoming, and the one in Mesquite, New Mexico."

There was a chair and desk in one corner and he went there to read the paper. There was still some light coming in through a window over the desk.

He read the accounts of both robberies, and they were much the same as the one in Heartless. In both cases the man had red hair and freckles and never made an attempt to cover his face. In Bekins no one was hurt, but in Mesquite a man was pistol-whipped, though not killed.

"Here's another," she said from behind him. He turned and accepted the paper, dated some five months ago. Same story.

"And another."

He took this one from her — dated a full year back — and asked, "Don't you have to cook for your grandfather?"

"He'll wait."

She provided him with nine newspapers in all, but told him that there were more robberies than that.

"I think there were twenty-three all told in two years," she said, "but these eighteen were the only ones committed at the same time."

"Apparently."

"What?"

"I said they were apparently committed at the same time by the same man." He touched the stack of papers on the desk and said, "We know that's impossible, though."

"Why is it impossible?"

He looked at her to see if her question was serious.

"Felicia, these robberies were all committed hundreds of miles apart. No one can be in two places at one time."

"Maybe," she said, "and maybe not. I have some ideas on the subject."

"How do you know so much about this? How were you able to pick these newspapers out so easily?"

"That was easy. I read everything I can about men like Foxx and Wild Bill Hickok.

33

I read dime novels, too."

"You do, huh?"

"Sure." A thought struck her. "Were there ever any dime novels about you?"

"Not that I know of."

"Decker, Decker . . ." she repeated, thinking. "No, I don't think so."

"Good," he said, standing up.

"Where are you going?"

"I'm finished here."

"Don't you want to hear my ideas?"

"Not right now, Felicia. I appreciate your help, but you'd better get on home and cook supper for your grandfather. He looks like he can use all the meals he can get."

"But I can help you —"

"You already have," he said, taking out two bits to give her.

"I don't want your money!" she snapped, backing away.

"Take it. It's the only way I have of thanking you."

"Go on, get out of here!" she shouted. "Big-shot bounty hunter, too big to let a girl help you."

He put the money down on a stack of papers and said, "Thanks, Felicia."

"Get out!"

He left feeling bad that she was angry. She'd been very helpful and he liked her.

Maybe he should have listened to her ideas. Maybe later. . . .

Chapter V

Brian Foxx was eating dinner when Brent Foxx walked through the door of the saloon.

"Hello, brother," Brent said.

"You're late."

His younger brother, dusty from the trail, dropped his gear to the floor next to the table.

From behind the bar the bartender stared at the two men. He'd seen them together before, but it never ceased to amaze him. They were identical! Same hair, same freckles, same build. If Brent hadn't been so dirty, he wouldn't have been able to tell them apart.

Or was the dirty one Brian?

"I got held up," Brent Foxx told his brother. "It's good to see you, too."

"Had to throw off a posse, you mean."

Brent gave Brian one of his little-boy looks.

"You heard."

"Did you have to kill somebody?"

Brent sat down and poured himself a drink from his brother's bottle, then grabbed a piece of meat from his plate with dirty fingers and stuffed it into his mouth.

"I don't kill unless I have to, Brian," Brent said. "You know that. He was gonna draw down on me. What was I supposed to do?"

Brian thought that was bullshit, but he didn't say so. There was no use in starting an argument, not now. He still had some talking to do first.

"Why don't you get cleaned up and then come back and have something to eat?" he suggested. "We've got some talking to do."

"Planning, you mean?"

"Yeah, planning."

"When do we pull our next jobs?' " Brent always asked that question with such eagerness.

"We don't."

"Whataya mean, we don't?"

"Get cleaned up and we'll talk about it." Brent was going to complain, but Brian said, "Go on."

"All right," Brent said, relenting. "I *could* use a bath." Brent turned to the barkeep and said, "Sam, a steak that thick. Okay?" He held his fingers apart to indicate how thick he wanted his steak.

"You got it."

Brent waved, then picked up his gear and went upstairs to his room.

Brian had decided while waiting for his brother that they were going to lay low for a while. This was the first time someone had gotten killed during a job, and that made it a special case.

Now all he had to do was convince his brother.

CHAPTER VI

After a late dinner, Decker went to the saloon again. This time he wanted a beer and a relaxing poker game. He'd gotten all he could get out of the witnesses and the sheriff, and it was time to start searching. He intended to travel a straight line from Heartless, Wyoming, to Doverville, Arizona, and see what popped up. He'd told the liveryman to have his horse ready at first light.

Tonight he wanted to relax because early the next morning he'd be on the trail again.

"You must like this place," the bartender said after he ordered a beer.

"It's the beer, not the company."

"Thanks loads."

"Any chance of a poker game?"

"If there is, you'll have to get it up yourself. I don't run any games in here."

"I'll take a table in the back. If anyone shows any interest, send them over, will you?"

"Sure."

"And make sure they have some money."

"Of course."

The man gave him a fresh deck of cards, and Decker took them to the table with him and put them right in the center, unopened.

Before long a couple of cowboys ambled over to his table and said, "We hear you're looking for a game."

"That's right."

"What stakes?"

"Just killing time."

"Sounds good to us."

"You fellas brothers?"

"Nope. We happened to be at the bar when the bartender asked if we were interested in the game," one man said, and the other nodded.

"Take a seat, gents," Decker said, reaching for the deck and thumbing the seal open, "the game is about to start."

CHAPTER VII

"Can we talk now?"

Brent Foxx stared across the table at his brother. He had just polished off a huge steak with some potatoes and biscuits and a pot of coffee. Now he poured himself a drink and addressed his brother.

"We've got to lay low for a while."

"Why?"

"Why? Because you killed somebody, that's why! 'Brian Foxx' is not just a bank robber anymore, he's a killer."

Brent shrugged.

"You're the one who wanted his name used."

"Nobody was ever supposed to get killed, Brent. We agreed. It's bad enough you like to beat up on people —"

"I explained all of that!"

"Never mind," Brian said. "I've already decided. We're not going to pull a job for a while. In fact, we're gonna pull up stakes and move east."

"East? To where?"

"Louisiana."

"New Orleans," Brent said knowingly.

"Yes. We pull our jobs in Arkansas and Missouri —"

"I don't want to go east, Brian. I like it here."

They locked eyes and Brian knew that if he flinched first he would be lost. It had become harder and harder to match his brother's mad stare lately. Finally Brent's eyes flicked away and then down to his plate.

"Sleep on the idea, Brent. We can talk about it in the morning."

"Sure, Brian," Brent said. "Sure." He stood up.

"Where you going?"

"I've been on the trail a long time. I need a woman. You coming?"

"No, you go ahead."

Brent paused and asked, "You mind if I use both girls?"

"You been on the trail that long?"

"Seems like it."

"Sure, they're all yours."

"Thanks. See you in the morning, Brian."

"Good night."

Brent left the saloon with a spring in his

step, like a little boy on his way to a candy store.

Sam came over, a small man in his thirties who had a special deal with the Foxx boys to provide them food and shelter whenever they showed up.

"Want another bottle?" he asked, claiming the empty.

"No, Sam. Thanks."

"Coffee?"

Brian thought a moment, then said, "Yeah, coffee."

He knew it was going to be one of those nights when he couldn't sleep.

Chapter VIII

Once the game started they quickly acquired two more players. They played for two hours, and at the end of that time Decker was up about a hundred dollars.

They were starting the third hour of play when the bat-wing doors opened and Felicia Wheeler walked in.

"Felicia —" the bartender said.

"Relax, Ted," she said, waving a hand at him. She surveyed the room until she spotted Decker and then hurried over to his table.

He saw her coming, but kept his eyes on his cards.

"Decker," she said.

He looked at her then.

"Shouldn't you be home in bed?"

"I went to the livery and saw your horse and gear," she said accusingly.

"So?"

"You said there had never been any dime

novels about you."

"There haven't, to my knowledge."

"But you didn't tell me who you really were!"

Decker lowered his cards and looked directly into her eyes.

"Go home, Felicia. We can talk tomorrow."

"That's a laugh. You're leaving early in the morning."

She must have gotten that from the liveryman.

"Felicia —"

"You didn't tell me you were the Hangman!"

"You're a hangman?" one of the players asked him curiously.

"No, I ain't," he said, annoyed now. "What the hell are you talking about, girl."

"You ride with a hangman's noose on your saddle, don't you?"

He felt all the eyes in the room fall on him, which he didn't like.

"I'm out of this game, gents," he said. He collected his money, stood up, and took Felicia by the ear.

"Good night, Decker," Ted the bartender called out. Decker waved his free hand and was aware of the laughter that filled the room as he led the girl to the door by her ear.

"Jesus, that hurts!" Felicia squawked, but Decker didn't release her until they were outside.

"Are you trying to get me killed?"

"What do you mean?" she asked, rubbing her ear.

"Any one of those men in there might have taken exception to who I was — and where the hell did you get this crap about me being called the Hangman?" he demanded.

"From this," she said, producing a curled-up book from her back pocket.

Decker took it, unfolded it, and looked at the cover. It showed a man on a horse with a hangman's noose hanging from the saddlehorn. At the top, in big letters, it said THE LEGEND OF THE HANGMAN.

"That's not me," he said, although he had to admit that looking at it made him uncomfortable.

"Then who is it?"

"This fella ain't even dressed like me," he said, indicating the painting on the cover.

"That's just the cover. You know anybody else who rides with a hangman's noose?"

"No," he admitted, "but this ain't about me. Is my name in there?"

"No. They call you Deacon in there. My grandfather says that's so you can't sue them."

He started to flip the pages, but there wasn't enough light for him to read by.

"Can I read this tonight?"

"You takin' it with you tomorrow?"

"No, I'll give it back — if you're at the livery at first light."

"All right," she agreed. "I'll be there — and if it's about you, you'll take me with you."

"I will not!"

"What kind of deal you making, then?"

"I'm not making any deal with a snot-nosed thirteen-year-old —"

"I'm fourteen!"

"All I'm doing is borrowing this book and meeting you at the livery in the morning. That's it. Take it or leave it."

She thought a moment, a stubborn look on her face, and then said, "All right, I'll take it."

"Then get your butt home and to sleep. You've got to get up early."

"You bet I will. I'm not letting you sneak off without seeing me."

Actually, the thought of sneaking away *had* occurred to him.

■ ■ ■ ■

Decker took the book to his room and read it, and he had to admit there were similarities between himself and the Hangman — not the least of which was the hangman's noose. According to the copyright page, it was published out of New York City. The similarities were such that it might make sense to go to New York and talk to the man who wrote it — this Ned Buntline, whoever he was — even if, as Felicia's grandfather had said, he couldn't sue them.

Then again, men like Decker rarely left it to a court of law to solve their problems.

He put the book aside, first making a note of the publisher's address. One of these days he'd get to New York and check on it.

Actually, the damned story in the book hadn't been bad at all.

CHAPTER IX

He got to the livery before the sun started to come up, and Felicia was there already.

"Good morning," he said, handing her the book.

"I saddled your horse for you."

"*You* did?"

"I told old Hiram to stay asleep."

Decker checked the cinch on his saddle and found that she had done a good job.

"Picked up your supplies for you, too."

"Did you, now?"

She nodded.

"Mr. Walker at the general store is friends with my grandfather."

Actually, Decker usually had coffee and jerky in his saddlebags and little else in the way of stores. He believed in traveling light and eating light. It made the first meal when you came off the trail taste that much better.

Felicia handed him a canvas sack, though,

and he accepted it.

"You got bacon and coffee, some jerky, some biscuits, and a can of peaches."

"Thanks."

"Sure."

He hefted the sack and said, "Not enough here for two."

She looked sheepish.

"That was silly of me, to think you'd take me with you."

"Yes, it was."

She touched the hangman's noose while he tied the sack to the back of his saddle.

"Did you read the book?"

"I did."

"What did you think?"

"It wasn't bad."

"But was it you?"

He turned and looked down at her. Her eyes were wide and shining, her nose pug with freckles on the bridge. She was going to be a beauty when she got older and filled out.

"No, Felicia, it wasn't me. I admit it was real close, but somebody's imagination is pretty good, is all."

"Mr. Buntline's."

"Yes."

"I have heard of you, though," she said, still touching the noose.

"Have you?"

"Or read about you, I should say. The bounty hunter who carries a hangman's noose on his saddle. I always wanted to ask you why."

"When you get a little older, I'll come back and tell you."

"Promise?"

"I promise."

"Great! And maybe then, if I'm pretty enough, you'll take me with you when you leave."

"You'll be pretty enough," he said, mounting up, "but we'll have to talk about that when the time comes."

"Wait," she said as he started to ride out. "Don't you want to hear my ideas?"

"I don't have time, Felicia."

He was riding away when he heard her shout out, "You're a fool if you don't realize that you're looking for two men!"

In Doverville, Arizona, a rider left town at first light the same day, traveling light. The intention of this rider was to ride in a straight line from Doverville to Heartless, Wyoming.

Decker made excellent time and crossed into Utah in three days. Ol' John Henry may have lacked the speed of younger horses, but his stamina was as good as ever.

Along the way he had not stopped in many towns. He was trying to put himself in Brian Foxx's place. The man had just pulled a bank robbery and would be looking for a place to light for a while — maybe even the same place after every job.

One thing Decker had learned about Brian Foxx was that his jobs — the "dual" jobs — were confined largely to Wyoming and Arizona, with an occasional foray into New Mexico.

Why not Utah?

Why not Colorado?

The answer was simple. Foxx's home between jobs was in one of those places, and Decker's immediate guess was Utah.

He also figured that Foxx wouldn't stop in any towns for supplies or whatever until he entered Utah. His face was too well-known to risk stopping in a Wyoming town, especially when he'd pulled a robbery so recently.

Men in Decker's profession often relied on hunches, and he had a hunch that Foxx was heading for a hole somewhere in Utah.

■ ■ ■ ■

PART TWO:
FOXX HUNT

■ ■ ■ ■

CHAPTER X

The first town Decker encountered in Utah was South Bend. It was rather small, but it might have been the right size for Foxx to stock up on supplies and take a night's rest in a real bed.

Decker left ol' John Henry in the hands of the liveryman and said, "I won't be staying long. I just want him to have some feed and a blow."

The man nodded and took the reins. When he saw the noose, he paused, but then continued without a word. Decker left his shotgun and saddlebags on the saddle and walked out.

He went to the saloon first for a beer to cut the dust, then went to the general store.

"Can I help you?"

"Yes," Decker said. He took a licorice stick from a glass bowl and said, "How much?"

"A penny."

He took two more and handed the man

a nickel.

"I'm looking for a friend of mine who might have passed through here."

"Is that so?" the man said, handing him the change.

"You couldn't miss him. Red hair and freckles like a kid, only he's no kid."

The man didn't reply. He was in his early forties and looked more like a ranch hand than a store clerk. Big shoulders, big hands with black hair on the backs of them.

"He might have come in here to stock up on some supplies. You might have waited on him."

"Can't say that I did," the man said.

"Maybe if you thought about it —"

"Can I get you something else, mister? If not, you're taking me away from my other customers."

Decker looked around and saw that the place was empty.

"What other customers?"

"They'll be along shortly."

"Uh-huh," Decker said. He decided not to push the man. "Thanks for the licorice."

"Don't mention it."

As he left the store, he saw a woman walking toward him holding a child by each hand, one a boy and the other a girl. They appeared to be about six or eight, and the woman looked to be in her early thirties, pleasant looking but no beauty.

"Excuse me, ma'am," he said, stepping in front of her. She caught her breath but relaxed when Decker handed each of the children a licorice stick.

"Do you like licorice, ma'am?"

"Very much," she said.

He handed her the last one, tipped his hat, and stepped into the street.

"What do you say?" he heard her ask the children.

"Thank you," they both called after him.

Decker waved a hand behind him and promptly forgot all three of them.

His next stop was the sheriff's office, where he hoped he wouldn't run into any more old, familiar faces.

He didn't.

"Excuse me, Sheriff."

The man behind the desk looked up, and Decker could see that he was being sized up. The lawman was about his age, but beefier, with big hands that had black hair on the backs of them.

"Can I help you?"

"You are the sheriff, aren't you?"

The man nodded.

"Sheriff Blocker."

"Well, Sheriff, my name is Decker. I'm looking for Brian Foxx, and I have reason to believe he may have passed through this town in the past two weeks or so."

"Bounty hunter?"

"That's right."

"There's no paper on Foxx in Utah."

"I know that."

"I haven't seen him."

"Would you tell me if you had?"

"No."

"Don't you want to see a wanted man brought to justice?"

"Not to your justice."

"I thought there was only one kind of justice."

"Bullshit. You're a bounty hunter, and *your* justice is not the same as mine."

Decker noticed that when he mentioned Foxx to people in this town they became belligerent.

"I'll be in town for a short time," he told the lawman. "I'll be leaving before evening."

"You should leave sooner than that."

"I'm giving my horse some rest, if you don't mind."

"I do, but I don't suppose there's anything I can do about it."

"I guess not."

Decker started for the door, but the sheriff

called out, "Decker."

"Yeah?"

"I wouldn't ask any questions about Brian Foxx in this town."

"Why not? Was he born here?"

"No, I just don't think people would take kindly to it."

"I'll keep that in mind, Sheriff."

"You do that."

Decker left and headed for the saloon. If there was one place Foxx would have definitely stopped, it was the saloon.

After Decker left the sheriff's office, the lawman stood up and walked to the window. He watched as Decker walked toward the saloon, then he left his office and crossed the street to the general store and went inside.

CHAPTER XI

When the first blow struck Decker in the stomach, he thought about the sheriff's warning.

He felt strong hands dragging him into an alley and tried to focus his eyes to see how many assailants there were. From the feel of it, there were definitely more than one.

In the alley he was hit again in the stomach, and he sagged against the wall of the saloon. While he was leaning there, somebody stepped in and hit him in the kidney, once, and then again, with a fist like a sledgehammer. He slid down the wall until he was lying on the ground. Then somebody else kicked him hard in the side and he started to cough.

He felt a hand tangle itself in his hair as his head was lifted off the ground.

"Stop asking questions about Brian Foxx and leave town." The voice was raspy and unrecognizable. "It'll be healthier for you."

In his condition he couldn't have recognized the voice even if he knew it, because his ears were ringing. When the hand released his head, however, he caught a quick glimpse of it. He got an impression of thick fingers and wiry black hair on the back of his hand.

Then he got kicked again and passed out.

Decker had entered the saloon a few minutes earlier, gone to the bar, and ordered a beer. He asked the bartender the same things he had asked the clerk in the general store.

"Red hair, you say?" the man said, frowning. "And freckles? A man like that should stay out of a place like this."

"Why's that?"

"A face like that is bound to start fights. Somebody has a little too much to drink and decides to pass a remark. You know how it is."

"Sure. Did you see him?"

"Nope."

"You'd remember if you had, right?"

"Sure."

"And you'd tell me?"

"Now why wouldn't I?"

"That's a good question."

He left the beer and started for the door.

"Hey, something wrong with the beer?"

As it turned out, it was a good thing he'd passed on the beer.

He surely would have thrown it up when the first punch struck him in the stomach.

He struggled to his feet and had to lean against the wall for support. He did that for a while, then pushed himself to a standing position and checked out his limbs. They all moved when he asked them to, and he took a few tentative steps without falling on his face. His stomach and side hurt, and his kidney ached, but aside from that he was in fairly good condition. His face had not been touched. It had been a very professional beating, administered by at least two men.

And he thought he knew one of them.

"You're accusing me?" the sheriff demanded.

Decker looked at the black hair on the back of the sheriff's hands again.

"Not accusing, exactly."

"In broad daylight?" the sheriff went on. "Of beating you up in my own town?"

"I just thought I'd ask, Sheriff," Decker said. "After all, we didn't hit it off right away, did we?"

"That's no reason for me to jump you and

beat you up. If I disliked you that much, I'd tell you to your face."

"Of course," Decker said, although he did not believe it for a moment.

"I warned you not to ask questions in this town," the sheriff said. "You'll remember that I warned you."

"Yes, you did warn me."

"Were you asking questions in the saloon?"

"Yes."

The sheriff spread his hands.

"That explains it, then."

"Does it?"

"Somebody overheard you in the saloon and didn't like the idea of you asking questions."

"Why should somebody object to my asking questions about Brian Foxx?"

"He's a well-known man, but like I said before, he ain't wanted in Utah. Maybe somebody just didn't like the idea of you hounding an innocent man."

"Innocent," Decker repeated.

"Mount up and ride out, Decker. It sounds like you were lucky this time."

Decker decided to play it a little differently.

"Yes, it does, doesn't it? You know something, Sheriff? I think I'll take your advice."

"Good. It'll be better for everybody concerned."

"Thanks for your help, Sheriff."

"My pleasure."

Decker looked at the man's hands again, then left. From the boardwalk in front of the sheriff's office, he looked across the street at the general store.

Sheriff Blocker was not the only man in town with large, hairy hands.

CHAPTER XII

Jerry Blocker was preparing to close his general store, taking in his wares from outside. He locked the front door and pulled the shade down. That done, he began carrying sacks of flour into his storeroom in the back. As he walked through the curtained doorway, he felt something tighten around his neck.

A rope pulled Blocker up onto his toes. Another inch and he'd be hanging.

"What —" He tried to speak but could only make choking noises.

"Hello, Blocker. Your name is Blocker, isn't it? The sheriff's brother?"

Off to his left Blocker could see the man who had been asking questions about Brian Foxx. Now he was leaning against the wall, holding a rope in his hand — the other end of the rope that was around Blocker's neck.

"I asked you a question," Decker said, yanking on the rope a fraction of an inch.

"Is your name Blocker?"

The man nodded.

"And you're the sheriff's brother?"

A shake of the head.

"Cousin, then?"

A nod.

"I guess hairy hands must run in your family, huh, Blocker?"

A nod.

"What's your name?"

The man tried to answer, but had difficulty getting it out.

"Go ahead," Decker encouraged him, loosening the rope just a bit. "It's just one word. You can get it out."

The man tried and finally managed to squeeze out his first name.

"Jerry!"

"All right, Jerry, you paid me a visit in the alley by the saloon, didn't you?"

Yes. Blocker went back to nodding and shaking his head.

"And the sheriff was with you?"

No.

"But he sent you, didn't he?"

Yes.

"And you brought help?"

Yes.

"One man?"

Yes.

Decker decided to let that go. The second man was very likely just a hireling, and it would be counterproductive for Decker to waste time finding him.

"You were supposed to warn me off and get me to leave town."

Yes.

"Now I'd like you to tell me why."

The man made strangling noises.

"I'm going to loosen the rope so you can talk, Blocker, but if I don't like your answer I'm going to string you up. You got that?'

The man nodded vigorously.

Decker eased up on the rope and pulled. The beam moaned in protest, but held, and Blocker was suddenly yanked off his feet. It was testimony to how Decker's slender appearance belied the strength he actually possessed.

Decker waited until the man's face was beet-red and then released the rope so that Blocker could slump to his knees.

"That wasn't smart, was it, Jerry?"

The man didn't answer.

"For one thing, you almost pulled down a beam. That would have brought your own roof down around your head. You wouldn't want that to happen, would you?"

No answer.

"Would you?" Decker asked, pulling up

on the rope again until the man's neck was stretched.

"No!" the man yelped.

"Okay, good. Let's get back to the question now, Blocker. Why is everyone so eager for me to stop asking questions about Brian Foxx?"

"The sheriff," Blocker said slowly, "my cousin. Him and Foxx are friends."

"Is that a fact? So that means that Foxx did come through here in the past two weeks."

"Yes."

"And you stocked him up on supplies."

"Yes."

"Enough for a long trip?"

When there was no answer, Decker pulled on the rope.

"Jesus, man, I'm thinkin', I'm thinkin'," the man shouted. "No, I wouldn't say he was gonna make that long a trip."

"Then he's staying in the Utah region?"

"That'd be my guess."

"Would the sheriff know where?"

"You'd have to ask him, but I'd say no. Foxx is too smart to let anybody know where he's gonna hole up."

"I think you're right, Blocker," Decker said. He walked over to the kneeling man and removed the noose from around his neck. "I want to thank you for your co-operation."

He coiled the rope as he walked for the front door. He had forced the back door in order to get in.

"Oh, and if you're planning on running over to the sheriff after I leave, don't bother. I'm going over there myself now."

"He won't be in his office," Blocker rasped.

"Oh, no?"

"He's got a woman in a house at the south end of town. He'll be there."

"Why are you telling me that, Jerry?"

The man glared at him and said, "Why should I be the only one to suffer?"

"Good point," Decker said, believing the man. "Tell me again where this house is . . ."

Decker's horse was saddled and waiting for him behind the general store. He rode to the south end of town and found the house Jerry Blocker had described to him. It was a one-story wooden structure with a falling-down wooden fence around it, and there was a light on in the back.

Decker walked around to a lighted window and looked in. Sheriff Blocker was in bed with a busty blonde, and they were so involved with each other that Decker thought they would hardly notice him even if he broke the window. He decided, however, to make his entry more discreetly.

He went to the kitchen door and popped the flimsy lock as quietly as possible. He entered, holding his rope in his left hand, and made his way toward the bedroom.

He paused at the door to survey the situation in the room. The sheriff was on top of the woman, humping away for all he was worth, his head held high as he strained with the effort.

Perfect.

Decker approached the bed, dangled the noose, and slid it over the sheriff's head. He pulled it tight, yanking the sheriff's head back even farther.

"Wha—" he said, but the rope tightening around his neck cut him off.

Decker pulled the sheet off the sheriff and wrapped the other end of the rope first around the man's wrists, securing them behind his back, and then his ankles, almost the way a cowhand ties a calf for branding. The sheriff's slightest move would cut off his own flow of air.

The woman, momentarily stunned, opened her mouth to scream, but Decker produced his gun and pointed it at her face, cocking it.

"Don't," he said.

The gun did its job, frightening her into silence. She was in her mid to late thirties, with a fleshy body that was very much in evidence now.

Talking about fleshy bodies, the sheriff was more than a few pounds overweight and resembled a full-grown cow rather than a calf, trussed up the way he was — and, Jesus, he had wiry black hair everywhere, not just on his hands.

"Just sit tight and you won't get hurt," Decker said to the woman.

She nodded, trying to hide her pale breasts with her hands. As an afterthought Decker picked the sheet up off the floor where he'd thrown it and tossed it to her.

"Thank you," she said, wrapping it around her.

The sheriff, meanwhile, was making an effort to speak and not having any luck.

"If you stop struggling," Decker told him, "you'll find that the rope is loose enough to allow you to talk."

The lawman struggled on, but when his face began to turn red he decided to take Decker's advice and relax, and he was able to breathe.

"You're a dead man, Decker," he rasped.

"Right now, Sheriff, you're closer to being

dead than I am." Decker went around to the sheriff's big behind, slid the barrel of his gun down along the crack in his ass, and then pushed it in just enough to startle him.

"H-Hey," the sheriff said.

"I'm going to ask you some questions, Sheriff, and if I don't like the answers, I'm going to pull the trigger. You'll have the biggest asshole in the Utah region."

Decker cocked the hammer on the gun, and the sheriff's entire body tensed.

"Hey, wait —"

"Question number one — do you know Brian Foxx?"

"Yes, yes, I know Brian Foxx. Look, Decker, take it easy —"

"Question number two — did he go through town in the past two weeks?"

"All right, yes, yes, he did. I had my cousin give him some supplies."

"The same cousin you had work on me earlier today?"

"Yeah — but, hey, that wasn't nothing personal, Decker, believe me —"

"Oh, I believe you, Sheriff, I really do. Now, here comes the third and most important question — do you know where Foxx was going?"

"No, h-honest, I don't. I only know that

he was going to hole up in the region somewhere."

"Is that the truth?" Decker asked, apply-
ing pressure to the gun.

"Yes, Jesus, yes, Decker, it's the truth!"

Decker believed him.

He eased the hammer down on the gun
and removed it. The rope he had used on
the sheriff was not his best one, so he
decided to leave it.

He holstered his gun and said to the
woman, "What's your name?"

"G-Gloria."

"Gloria, after I'm gone you can untie your
boyfriend, but I want you to count to fifty
first, okay?"

"Y-Yes."

"And you won't let him talk you into
untying him sooner? I can trust you?"

"Y-Yes, yes."

Decker slapped the sheriff on his hairy
rump hard enough to leave an imprint of
his hand, and then leaned over to speak into
the man's ear.

"Now, Sheriff, I know this must have been
very embarrassing for you, but I want you
to remember something. If I hear that
you've put out any paper on me, I'm going
to come back and finish what I started. Do
you understand?"

"I understand, all right," the lawman said, "but believe me, Decker, you won't be around long enough for me to put a poster out on you. Foxx will see to that. If I knew where he was, I'd tell you just so he could kill you."

"Well, I appreciate that, Sheriff, I really do." Decker turned to the woman and said, "Gloria, you take good care of our boy, all right?"

"Y-Yes, I w-will."

"Good night."

Decker walked through the house, out the kitchen door, and mounted up. He didn't expect the woman to be able to count all the way to fifty. In fact, he could already hear the sheriff shouting at her. Still, he didn't think the sheriff would come after him. He would leave things to Brian Foxx.

And that was just fine with Decker.

Chapter XIII

Brian and Brent Foxx were sitting across from each other in the saloon in Fenner's Fork. They had been sitting like that for some time now, and the bartender, Sam, was leaning on the bar, watching them both with interest.

"What are we gonna do, sit here forever?" Brent asked Brian.

"We can't agree on a course of action, Brent," Brian said. "That means we can't *take* a course of action, can we?"

"Sure we can."

"What?"

"I passed a town on the way here that's got a bank that's ripe. One of us could go back and pull the robbery off easy."

"It's too soon, Brent," Brian said, shaking his head. "It's not safe."

"When has anything we've ever done been safe?" Brent said. "I don't agree."

"And that's why we're sitting here staring

at each other, isn't it?" Brian asked. "Because we can't agree."

"I don't want to leave this area, Brian," Brent said stubbornly.

"And I do," Brian said. "I know it's the right move to make, Brent, and we're gonna stay in this town until I can convince you of that."

"In that case," Brent said, waving to Sam, "I need another drink."

Brent got up to get the drink and Brian watched his brother's retreating back. He could feel the split coming, and he didn't want it to happen. If they separated, he knew that Brent would make a mistake and get caught or be killed.

He couldn't let that happen — but how was he going to stop it?

Chapter XIV

Decker knew a little about the Utah region, especially the fact that it was short on water. He usually carried an extra canteen, and while he was in Utah it would come in even more handy than usual.

He knew that the early settlers of Utah were the Mormons, and that they had emigrated from New York by way of Missouri, Ohio, and Illinois. They were not welcomed in those places because of the peculiarities of their religion — not the least of which was the fact that men were allowed more than one wife — and for that reason they had decided to try and settle in Utah.

He knew that when the Mormons first came to Utah it had been owned by Mexico, but that it had since passed into the hands of the United States. Statehood, however, had been denied it, again because of the religious beliefs of its prime inhabitants. Salt Lake City had been the headquarters of the

Mormons since 1847, but Decker did not foresee getting to that part of the region.

Indian problems — mostly with the Utes — had been solved as early as 1857, and the Utes were presently on a reservation.

Utah was peaceful now, but animosity still existed between the Mormons and the outside world, which would prevent Utah from becoming a state of the Union for years to come.

Two days after leaving the town of South Bend, Decker was certain that the sheriff had not gathered a posse and was not on his trail.

Seven days out of the town he suddenly became aware that somebody *was* on his trail, but whether or not the person was from South Bend was another story.

Ten days and he was still being trailed, although whoever it was had not chosen to close the distance between them.

Decker decided it was time to find out who was following him.

That night, instead of camping, Decker started a fire, then moved into the darkness and mounted John Henry. He started to backtrack, testing the air for signs of a campfire. Finally he caught the scent of coffee and followed it. When he felt he was getting nearer the fire, he dismounted and left John Henry standing alone, untethered. He knew the old gelding was not going anywhere, and he wanted the horse to be able to respond to a whistle.

He crept closer to the campfire and saw somebody hunkered down by the fire, his back to him. Off to the right a horse was picketed, a big gray mare. Decker moved into the circle of light quietly and, approaching the figure, discovered how small the person was. He left his gun in his holster and decided to just use his hands.

He grabbed the man around the chest and straightened up, lifting him up off his feet.

"All right, friend, let's have a talk."

The man kicked and struggled and then said, "You ain't lettin' me breathe, damn it!"

Startled, Decker opened his arms and let his captive drop to the ground. The voice had not been a man's but a woman's — or more to the point, a girl's.

Felicia Wheeler.

"Damn you, Decker," she swore, getting to her feet, "you trying to kill me?"

"You little whipper!" he said, staring at her. "What the hell are you doing dogging my trail — and if you swear again I'll cuff you."

"You —" she said, and cut herself off.

"Come on, explain yourself."

"I want to be there when you find Brian Foxx."

"Why?"

"Two reasons. I told you I'm interested in people like him — and you. I want to see who comes out on top."

"And the second reason?"

"When it happens, I want to write about it."

"Write about it?"

"But not for my grandfather's paper. Nobody would see it. I want to write about it and send it to someplace big — someplace like Denver, or San Francisco . . . or maybe even New York."

"And you've been following me all this time?"

"I followed your trail to South Bend, and then trailed you from there for a few days until I spotted you and laid back. You ain't found nothing yet, have you?"

"No — except you, and you're going home."

"I am not!"

"What about your grandfather?"

"Grandpa can eat out for a while. All he

lets me do is cook and clean."

"Isn't that what a woman is supposed to do?"

"Well, at least you admit I'm a woman!"

"Half a woman, anyway."

"I'm fourteen!"

"Like I said, half a woman. All right, come on."

"Where?"

"Gather up your stuff. We'll go to my camp and spend the night there. In the morning you'll start back."

"I ain't."

"You will or you'll wish you had."

"Why?"

"Because you'll run your ass off trying to keep up with me."

"I can travel as fast as you can."

"Is that so?"

"Yeah."

"Well, let's collect your gear, junior. You just might get a chance to prove that."

When they got back to his fire, they reheated her coffee and each had a cup.

"What are you gonna do when you find Foxx?"

"Take him in."

"Where?"

"Wherever we're closest to where he's

wanted."

"Did you think any about what I said back in town when you left?"

He knew what she meant, and he really hadn't thought about it that much.

"Two men, Decker. Think about it. How else could they pull jobs in different places at the same time?"

"But they'd have to look the same."

"You never heard of twins?"

"Twins!" He shook his head. "That's farfetched, Felicia. You been reading too many dime novels."

"Then you explain it."

"It might be two men, one made up to look like Brian Foxx."

"Made up?"

"Like an actor."

"But how would they be identical? Wouldn't somebody notice *something* different?"

"Maybe they're not identical. All we have are some physical descriptions to go on. Lots of people can sound identical that way."

"Why don't you want to admit that I might be right?"

He frowned, not liking the idea that she might be right. Twins! It sounded silly.

"You'd better get some rest, youngster,"

he said, instead of answering. "I'm gonna run your tail off tomorrow."

She grinned and said, "You'll try, but don't forget, I tracked you this far."

As she rolled up in her blanket, he admitted to himself that he was pretty damned impressed with this fourteen-year-old — and a girl, at that!

Chapter XV

Decker upped his pace the next day to try and tire out Felicia and the mare she called Nellie.

When they mounted up that morning, Felicia cast a critical eye John Henry's way.

"He must have been a fine horse in his time," she said.

"He's a fine horse anytime."

"He's a little old, don't you think? What is he, about eleven? Twelve?"

"He's nine."

"And he's a little small."

"He's big enough."

"I don't think he'll be able to keep up with Nellie."

Decker mounted up and said to her, "Shut up and ride."

Felicia was a surprise to Decker. She was able to keep up most of the way and never complained about the pace.

When they camped for dinner, Felicia

volunteered to make it if Decker would build the fire. They went about their chores and eventually were seated around the fire, eating bacon, beans, and biscuits with coffee.

During the meal Felicia tossed an admiring look John Henry's way.

"I'm sorry about what I said about John Henry this morning."

"He doesn't mind," Decker assured her. "He enjoys proving people wrong."

"Doesn't he ever get tired?"

"He could probably go all day if I'd let him, but I let him rest a spell every now and then. Nellie's not too bad, either," he said.

"Really?"

"She keeps up with him better than most."

"My pa gave her to me when I was ten. She was just two then. I guess she's no youngster either, huh? She's six."

"She'll last you a long time, don't you worry. Just remember to treat her right."

"Do you treat John Henry right? I've never seen you pet him or anything."

"He doesn't need petting. We both know our jobs and we do 'em. He knows I'll feed him and rest him and make sure he's taken care of, and he takes care of me in return."

"Nellie needs a lot of affection."

"Like most women."

"Have you known a lot of women?"

He stopped chewing for a moment and said, "Some."

"I'll bet you've known a lot."

"You better finish your dinner."

"Am I embarrassing you?"

"No, damn it, I just want to finish eating."

After a few moments of silence, she asked, "Do you think I'm pretty? I mean, back in town you said I was pretty enough, but do you really think I'm pretty?"

"You're pretty, Felicia, pretty enough to know it yourself. Don't go fishing for compliments. It isn't polite."

"I guess not, but I think you're very attractive, and if you wanted to . . . you know, sleep with me tonight, I'd let you."

He was sipping his coffee and started to choke on it.

"Jesus Christ, girl, don't do that to a man when he's drinking something."

"Are you all right?"

"I'm fine," he said, brushing wet coffee off his shirt front. "What the hell did you want to go and say a thing like that for anyway?"

"I was just telling you it's all right —"

"You're only fourteen years old, too young to sleep with anyone, let alone me."

"You mean you don't want to?"

"No, I don't want to," he said, still annoyed and not realizing that the words might hurt her.

"You don't think I'm a woman, do you? Well, I'll show you —"

As she started to unbutton her shirt, he reached over to grab her hands.

"Now sit still and be quiet for a few minutes and we'll talk about this."

She pulled her hands away and set them in her lap.

"Now, you know you're a pretty gal, and I know it, but as for you being a woman, that's not quite true, is it?"

She didn't answer.

"You're real close to being a woman, though. You've already filled out enough and you'll fill out even more in the next couple of years, but don't be throwing yourself at any man until you know what you're getting yourself into."

She still didn't answer, but he could feel her attitude changing from anger to embarrassment.

"I'm a lot older than you, Felicia. When the time does come, you'll want to give yourself to someone closer to your own age."

"You're not that old."

"I'm twice your age, and believe me that's

87

a big difference."

"All right."

"All right, what?"

"All right . . . I'll wait until I get a little older before I make that offer again."

Decker thought that over a few seconds and then said, "Well, all right."

"Can I ask you something?"

"What?" Decker asked warily.

"Why do you carry the hangman's noose?"

"That was one thing that dime novel of yours didn't mention, was it?"

"No, but that wasn't you anyway."

"Now you believe that?"

She gave him a half smile and said, "Now that I know you better, I can see for myself."

"Well, that's good."

"So?"

"So what?"

"So why do you carry the noose?"

"You sure ask a lot of questions."

"It's the only way I can get any answers. Besides, a good newspaper reporter has to know how to ask questions."

"That's what you want to be? A reporter?"

"More than anything. When Ma and Pa died of the fever, Grandpa took me in, and I been around the newspaper business ever since. You're changing the subject."

"You're right," Decker said, reaching for

the coffeepot, "I am."

"Well, if you don't want to answer, just say so."

He studied her over his new cup of coffee for a few moments and then asked, "You don't intend to write this down anywhere, do you?"

She hesitated, and then said, "Not until you tell me I can. I swear it."

"All right. It's very simple, really. . . ."

CHAPTER XVI

"It happened in Kansas when I was about twenty-one. A woman was killed and I was blamed."

"Why?"

"Well, I worked for her, doing odd jobs, and she showed an interest in me. She was older than me by about ten years, and married, and I didn't want to have anything to do with her."

"Was she pretty?"

"She was beautiful, but that was besides the point. Her husband had hired me to work, and that's what I wanted to do. Anyway, she got mad at me and told her husband I tried to . . . touch her, so he fired me."

That was an oversimplification. Decker and the man had a big fight, during which Decker knocked the man down in front of his wife. Doubly embarrassed, the man fired Decker and never paid him the money he owed him. That was fine with Decker, though. He just wanted to get away from the two of them.

"I was leaving town on foot when the posse rode up and arrested me for killing her."

Actually, they arrested him for raping her and then killing her.

"But why you?"

"The husband told them I did it."

"Was there any proof?"

"The case got all the way to court. A judge, eager to make a name for himself with a sensational case, convicted me on flimsy evidence."

The sheriff of the town, a man named Mike Farrell, had believed Decker to be innocent, but Decker was convicted and sentenced to hang.

Even now Decker could feel the noose around his neck.

"I got as far as the gallows, with the hangman putting the noose over my neck, before Mike Farrell brought the real killer in and made him confess."

"Who was it?"

"Her husband."

"What happened?"

"Apparently I wasn't the first one that she had thrown herself at, and that, combined with the fact that I knocked him down in front of her, made him mad enough to attack his own wife. I don't know if he meant to kill her, but he did, after raping her."

"And what happened to you?"

"The hangman took the noose off my neck and untied my hands and walked away."

"No apology?"

"Nobody apologized. When I walked down off the gallows, nobody was even there anymore. They'd gone home disappointed that they weren't going to see a hanging."

"And the sheriff?"

"He resigned and left town, and I rode with him for a short time. He tried to get me to take up being a lawman, but I had other ideas."

"Bounty hunting?"

"For a reason. I want to be able to get to the ones who are going to be hanged and satisfy myself that they're guilty before I hand them over. I don't want what happened to me to happen to any other innocent men."

"And the noose?"

"The noose is a reminder of what almost happened to me, and why I took up bounty hunting. I lose sight of my reasons once in a while, and the noose brings it back to me."

"Does that mean you won't bring Brian Foxx in unless you're convinced of his guilt?"

"That's what it should mean, but I've been finding myself already convinced. I mean, the eyewitness descriptions are pretty damaging."

"Which ones?"

Decker stared at her and then sipped his coffee. It had grown cold while he told his story. He dumped it into the fire and poured another cup.

"You're right, Felicia. Maybe I need more than the noose to remind me of my reasons."

"Does that mean we can be partners?"

He stifled a grin and said seriously, "Let's not get carried away."

Later, after they had retired, Felicia said, "Decker?"

"What?"

"Are you asleep?"

"No."

"What about the gun?"

"What gun?"

"The one you wear."

"I told you, I'm not very good with a handgun."

"Did you try to learn?"

"Mike Farrell was pretty good with a gun, and he tried to teach me, but it was hopeless, so he brought —"

"Wait a minute," she said, sitting up. "Mike Farrell. I know that name."

"Yeah, Mike went on to make a pretty good name for himself as a federal marshal."

"He's had dime novels written about him. 'Iron Mike' Farrell they call him."

"I guess. Anyway, he took me to a gunsmith friend of his and asked the man to design something for me that wouldn't require that I aim. That's when he came up with this rig."

"You and Iron Mike Farrell," Felicia said, with more than a little awe in her voice. "Decker, do you know Wild Bill Hickok."

"Felicia."

"Yeah?"

"Go to sleep."

CHAPTER XVII

The next afternoon they came within sight of a ranch house. There was a barn that was in a state of disrepair, and a corral with a few horses in it, but beyond that it didn't look like much of a spread.

"Are we going to stop?" Felicia asked.

"To water the horses and ask some questions."

Felicia moved as if to go forward, and Decker put his hand on her arm to stay her.

"We don't know who's down there, Felicia, and so far my questions have not been well received."

"You want me to watch you closely, right?"

"Right."

"Okay."

"I'll go first."

Decker urged John Henry on and Felicia fell in behind them.

As they approached the ranch house, the front door opened and a man stepped out.

He was followed by a woman, and then a girl.

The man appeared to be in his midforties, solidly built, his black hair flecked with gray and cut short. He had a solid jaw and a thin slit of a mouth. The woman was about thirty-five, handsome and well-shaped, with dark hair pinned up in a bun. The girl was no more than seventeen or so, slender and blonde, her hair worn long and loose. She was very lovely.

"Can I help you?" the man asked.

At that point Decker veered John Henry to his right, and the people on the porch became aware of Felicia.

"John . . ." the woman said, putting her hand on the man's arm. Decker assumed that they were husband and wife, and that the girl was their daughter.

"My name is Decker," he said, "and this is Felicia."

"Is she your daughter?" the woman asked.

"No, ma'am, we're just traveling together."

"For what purpose?" the man asked.

"I'm looking for someone," Decker said. "A red-haired man who may have passed this way within the past two weeks."

"And the girl?"

Decker looked at Felicia, who remained silent.

"She's a newspaper reporter, looking for a story."

"Is that right?" the man said. He looked at Felicia and said, "You seem so young."

"I'm fourteen, and Mr. Decker is making fun of me. My grandfather has a newspaper, and I *want* to be a reporter. I followed Mr. Decker from Wyoming because I think he'll make a good story."

"Followed him?"

"She trailed me and eventually caught up with me. She's very determined."

"So it would seem," the man said. The woman leaned over and said something into his ear, and the man nodded. "My wife would like to ask that you step down and have lunch with us. We would be most pleased if you would accept."

Felicia looked at Decker, who nodded.

"We're grateful, ma'am," he said to the woman.

"Would you like to put your horses in the barn?"

"Thank you."

"Why doesn't the young lady come inside with us," the woman suggested, "while you and my husband take care of the horses."

"All right," Decker said, and Felicia stepped down.

"This way," the man said, taking the reins

97

of Felicia's horse and leading the way to the barn.

Inside the barn, as they unsaddled the horses, the man said, "My name is John Hudson."

"I'm grateful to your wife for the offer. I've been trying to get Felicia to return home. Your daughter is not much older than she is. Maybe she can help me persuade —"

"Sara is not my daughter," John Hudson said. "She is my wife."

"I'm sorry," Decker said, "I thought the other woman —"

"Esther is also my wife."

Decker pulled the saddle from John Henry's back and shifted it to a post, where he balanced it.

"We are Mormons," Hudson said.

Hudson turned to face Decker.

"You do not disapprove?"

"It's not my place to disapprove, Mr. Hudson."

"Please, call me John. Let us go and have lunch."

"Sounds good."

They watered and fed the horses and then Decker followed Hudson to the house, trying not to judge or disapprove. The way these people wanted to live their lives was up to them.

At least the man had good taste in wives.

Decker followed Hudson into his house, where he was assailed by delicious odors. Apparently one or both of his wives could cook as well.

Felicia hurried to Decker's side and hissed, "They're Mormons."

Decker shushed her.

They all sat down to lunch. Felicia sat next to Sara. The women did most of the talking until John Hudson finally spoke, at which time his wives dutifully fell silent.

"This man you are after, is it Brian Foxx?"

"It is."

"Are you a lawman?"

"No, I'm a bounty hunter."

"I see. You are after the man for the price on his head."

"That's part of it," Felicia said.

Hudson looked at Felicia as if she had committed some great transgression.

"Please," Sara said to her, "we must remain silent while the men talk."

"Like hell —"

"Felicia!" Decker said.

She flashed him a defiant look, but stayed quiet.

"What does she mean?"

"Nothing. I'm after Foxx to bring him in for crimes he's committed. That's all you need to know."

"I see," Hudson said. Decker felt that he had probably insulted the man and would get no help at all now.

"Of course, you are correct," Hudson said. "It is then left to me to decide whether I want to help you or not. I disapprove of your profession, but I realize that Brian Foxx must be brought to justice."

"Well, I haven't met many people from Utah who agree with that."

"That is because he has not practiced his profession in this region, but the time will come when he will. He must be stopped before then."

"He did pass this way, then?" Decker continued.

"Yes."

"Did you give him a horse?"

"In exchange for his. We also gave him some food. He did not offer to pay, but we would not have taken it even if he had."

The man's tone clearly stated that Foxx *should* have offered and given them the opportunity to refuse.

"Did you see which way he went when he left?"

"He was traveling south when he came here, and continued in that direction."

"What's in that direction?"

Hudson shrugged. "Wide open spaces, mountains —"

"Where would Foxx hide out, John?"

"Are you asking me to think like a thief?"

"I'm asking you to try. I'm assuming you know this area."

"Very well. I chose to build my home here because it was isolated."

"Then pick a place."

Hudson thought a moment.

"There's a rock formation not far from here. I seem to remember a couple of towns at its base, one on the east side, one on the west. They'd be perfect . . . hideouts."

"And they're south of here?"

"Yes."

"We'll head that way, then," Decker said, standing up.

"Are you leaving now?" Esther asked.

"I want to cover more ground before it gets dark. We've really appreciated your hospitality."

"We've enjoyed the company," Sara said. She obviously meant Felicia. She was three years older than the other girl, but they seemed to have gotten on well, and Felicia *was* the closest person in the room to Sara's age.

As Felicia stood up, Sara put her hand on her arm.

"Why don't you stay with us?"

Esther looked at Decker and said, "The child would be welcome."

"I'm not a child!"

Esther smiled and said to Decker, "She would be welcome anyway."

Esther and Sara looked at their husband for his approval, and he nodded.

"That leaves it up to you," Esther said to Decker.

"Not me," he said. "It's up to Felicia."

"And I'm not staying," she said, moving to Decker's side. "I mean, I appreciate the offer, but I have to go with Decker."

"As you wish," John Hudson said.

"Let me pack you some food," Esther said, and Sara helped her fill a sack.

Hudson went to the barn with Decker and helped him saddle the horses. When they returned to the porch, each of Hudson's wives hugged Felicia and wished her well.

Decker and Felicia mounted up, waved, and rode south.

When they were out of sight of the ranch, Felicia said, "They were nice people."

"Yes."

"I can't understand their ways, though. I asked Sara how she could marry a man so much . . . older than she is."

"And?"

"She said she considered it an honor that he wanted her." Shaking her head, Felicia said, "I don't ever think I could be a Mormon. Imagine, not being able to talk while your husband is talking."

"Yes," Decker said, "having to be that obedient would be a strain, wouldn't it?"

Chapter XVIII

"All right," Brent Foxx finally said, "I'm tired of sitting here doing nothing. We've been here a week and nothing's been accomplished."

"Which means?" Brian asked.

"Which means we can either split up, or I can go your way. Those seem to be my only two choices."

"Brent —"

"Then again, *you* only have two choices. We could split up, or you could go my way."

"Brent —"

"I know, I know, you're the older brother, the big brain. You've made all the decisions up to now, and we've done all right."

Brian decided to keep quiet and let his brother work it out. He poured himself another drink and waited.

"Well, I guess if I go with you we can at least keep this scam going. It's worked too well up to now to let it just die. Of course, poor Sam here will be out of business if we leave."

"We'll pay him enough to keep him going until he can get himself another setup. There are always men on the run looking for a place to hide out."

"And the girls?"

"We'll give them some money, too."

"I was kind of hoping to take the cute one along."

"That kind of trouble we don't need."

"You're right. I guess one more night with her will have to do it. Will you be ready to leave tomorrow?"

"In the morning," Brian said.

"Fine. I'll go and give the ladies the bad news. Will you be over later?"

Brian nodded.

"See you later, brother." Brent started for the door and then stopped and turned. "I'm glad we got this all worked out."

"So am I, Brent."

As Brent left the saloon, Brian poured himself another drink. He was genuinely glad that it had been worked out amiably — but he was concerned that it had come *too* easily. His brother had something up his sleeve, and it made Brian nervous as hell.

On his way to see the two girls, Brent was

glad he had finally figured out a way to break the stalemate that had existed between his brother and himself. Brian had always been the boss, and that had been fine when they were younger, but Brent was older now and he thought that it was time he started thinking for himself.

Chapter XIX

As darkness started to fall, they came to a fork in the road. Ahead of them Decker could see the rock formation Hudson had told him about. It was several hundred feet high, coming to a peak at the top and then widening out as it came down.

They stopped at the fork and looked at the two crudely made signs. One said: FENNER'S FORK and pointed to the left fork, or the east one, and the other said: EATON'S FORK and pointed right, or west.

"What do we do now?" Felicia asked.

"We'll camp off the road a ways and in the morning we'll pick a fork."

They rode about fifty yards off the road and camped in a dry gully.

"Why here?"

"I don't want to take a chance on being seen from the road, just in case someone is traveling at night."

They took care of the horses, then Decker

told her there'd be no cooking that night.

"We'll build a small fire, but I don't want the scent of coffee or bacon giving us away."

"Well, let's see what the Hudsons gave us in the sack."

She began pulling out food.

"Cold chicken, some cans of fruit, some biscuits. With this, who needs hot food?"

They had their dinner and laid out their bedrolls.

"Decker?"

"What?"

"Did you want me to stay with the Hudsons?"

"No." His answer came without hesitation.

"Why not?"

"I didn't want to see you become wife number three."

"Oh, God!" she said. "There's no chance of me ever marrying a Mormon."

"Or an older man."

"Well, not somebody a *lot* older, anyway."

"Go to sleep."

"I'm not sleepy."

"I am."

"No you're not," she said. "You're never sleepy. I've never met anybody like you."

"I'm just a man."

"Decker," she said, "when you lie down

and close your eyes — I mean, when you *decide* that you're going to sleep — you're asleep like that. Then in the morning when you wake up, you open your eyes and you're awake right away. You don't even rub your eyes! That's not normal."

"It is for me."

"See? You're not normal."

"Well, neither are you."

"What do you mean?"

"Fourteen-year-old girls should not be traveling with bounty hunters. They should be home going to school, cooking for their grandfathers, and having boyfriends their own age."

"Boys my own age are . . . boys."

"They're supposed to be."

"Yech!"

"Felicia."

"Yes?"

"I've just decided to go to sleep."

And he did.

While Decker slept, Felicia watched him. If, as he had said, he was twice her age, that made him twenty-eight.

Sara had told her that she was seventeen, and that her husband John was forty-four. As far as Felicia was concerned, twenty-seven years was just too big a difference.

But it made fourteen years look like nothing at all!

On the south side of the rock formation was another camp, where one person dined on beef jerky.

In the morning a choice would be made as to which fork to take.

The east or the west.

A lot would depend on the decision.

Chapter XX

In the morning Decker and Felicia mounted up and faced the fork.

"Right," Decker said.

"Why?"

"Because we've got to choose one, and if I had said left, you would have asked why."

"And you would have given me the same answer. Okay — right."

They took the right fork, heading for Eaton's Fork.

At the south end of the formation the identical decision was made. To head left, to Eaton's Fork.

Eaton's Fork was a ghost town.

"Nothing's moved here for years," Felicia said as they rode down the main street.

"We'll have to check it out before we decide we've made the wrong choice and double back."

Decker was glad that Felicia had the good sense not to point out that the decision was his.

They stopped in front of what had been the saloon and dismounted.

"Stay here."

Decker went inside and immediately knew they were in the wrong place. Layers of dust covered everything. There were full bottles on some of the shelves behind the bar. If anyone had been here, it would have been impossible to hide his presence. There was no guarantee that Fenner's Fork wouldn't be the same way, but they were going to have to check it out.

He stepped back outside and knew something was wrong. Felicia was standing too stiffly.

"What is it?"

Felicia looked to his right and he followed her eyes and saw the gun.

"Where is Brian Foxx?" the woman holding the gun asked.

The woman was tall, full-bodied, apparently in her twenties. It was also apparent that she had traveled a long way and was looking for the same thing he was.

"He's not here."

"Don't bullshit me," the woman said.

"Go inside and check for yourself." He

looked at Felicia and said, "Mount up. We're going to have to double back and check the other place."

"Don't move!" the woman said.

Decker looked at her again. She had long auburn hair that tumbled to her shoulders from beneath a beat-up white Stetson. Cleaned up she'd be beautiful.

"Look. I've already checked inside and I don't have time to play games. I'm looking for Brian Foxx, too, and if I want the reward money I guess I'm going to have to find him before you do."

"You don't ride with him?"

"Hell, no."

She squinted at him and said, "Bounty hunter?"

"That's right."

"And her?"

"Meet the world's youngest newpaper reporter. This young lady is looking for a story. Would you like us to give her one here and now?"

"What do you mean?"

"I mean put that gun away before I take it away from you. You've already had it out long enough without using it. Its value has gone way down."

"Look," the woman said, obviously nervous, "how do I know I can believe you?"

From inside his shirt pocket Decker took out Foxx's poster. He unfolded it and held it out to the woman. As she came closer and reached for it, he dropped it and grabbed her wrist. He spun her around so that she was facing the other way and pulled her to him, then clamped his other hand down on her gun hand. He took the gun away from her and pushed her aside.

"He's telling the truth," Felicia said to the woman. She mounted the boardwalk, picked up the poster, and handed it to the woman.

"He really is a bounty hunter. His name is Decker."

"Let me do the introductions, please, Felicia," Decker said. "What's your name?"

"Rebecca Kendrick," the woman said, rubbing her wrists.

"Why are you looking for Brian Foxx?"

"He killed my brother in Doverville, Arizona, when he robbed the bank."

"And you trailed him this far?"

The woman nodded, still massaging her wrists.

"Look," Decker said, "I'm sorry if I hurt you." He held her gun out to her and she eyed him suspiciously. "Go on, take it and put it away. We have some talking to do."

She took the gun and holstered it.

"Do you want to check inside?"

"No," Rebecca Kendrick said. "I'll take your word for it."

"Where's your horse?"

"Back a couple of streets."

"Let's get it and get moving. We've got to get to Fenner's Fork."

"What do we have to talk about?" she asked as they walked. Felicia had mounted Nellie and was leading John Henry along behind them.

"I've been trailing Brian Foxx from a town called Heartless, Wyoming. He pulled a bank robbery there on the same day your brother was killed."

"But that's impossible. Witnesses saw him in Doverville."

"And witnesses saw him in Heartless."

"But how could that be?"

As they reached her horse, Decker said, "Well, my *partner* here has a theory . . ."

They doubled back the way Decker and Felicia had come, Decker and Rebecca riding side by side. Felicia rode behind them, fuming. She didn't like Rebecca Kendrick because she was so damn pretty.

"Twins," Rebecca said, shaking her head. "I can't believe that."

"I don't quite buy it either, but it is an interesting theory," Decker said. "It would explain how they do it."

"If there are two of them," Rebecca said, "how am I supposed to know which one to kill?"

"Well," Decker said, "it doesn't really matter, does it? You kill one and I'll take the other one in for the reward."

"You're making fun of me."

"Are you so sure you're going to kill him?"

"He killed my brother."

"All that means is that we know *he* can kill. The question is, can you?"

After a moment of silence, Rebecca said, "I really don't know."

"At least you're honest."

"But I've come all this way. . . ."

She explained to Decker that her strategy was simply to travel in a straight line in the same direction that "her" Brian Foxx had taken. He didn't comment on the fact that an amateur had come up with the same strategy as he'd used — and he was a professional.

It was too embarrassing.

It was midday when they rode into Fenner's Fork, and it didn't look any better than Eaton's Fork had, except for one thing — one of the buildings had smoke coming from the chimney.

"Well, at least somebody's here," Decker said.

"Let's take a look," Rebecca said.

"Hmph," Felicia said, but nobody heard her.

They rode over to the building and found that it was the saloon.

"More and more encouraging," Decker said.

They dismounted and Decker told Felicia to stay outside and hold the horses.

He looked at Rebecca and asked, "Can you do anything with that gun besides point it?"

"If I have to."

"That's a distinct possibility. You might want to wait out here with Felicia."

"I'm going inside with you, Mr. Decker."

Decker grimaced and said, "Just Decker."

Decker approached the batwing doors, drawing his weapon. He passed through the doors quickly and stepped to his right, swinging the sawed-off back and forth to cover the room. He was pleased to see that Rebecca came in right on his heels and moved to her left, gun drawn.

"Hey!" the bartender said, putting his hands up. "If you ain't got the money, it's on the house."

Decker's eyes took in the whole room and

it was empty.

"What's your name?" he asked.

"Sam."

"Anybody else here, Sam?"

"Here in the saloon, or here in town?"

"Answer both."

"Nobody else here, but there's a few people in the town. Couple of girls over in the hotel, if you're interested." Sam looked past Decker at Rebecca and added, "Although I don't see why you would be."

"Has there been anyone else here in the past couple of weeks?"

"Well, let's see —"

Decker had an instinct he trusted. It told him when somebody was going to lie to him, and it was talking to him now. He let go one barrel of the sawed-off and took out most of the liquor bottles on the man's right. The bartender ducked, but couldn't avoid the shower of whiskey and glass that fell on him like baptismal water.

"Hey!" he shouted.

"Mister, I don't care how much they paid you," Decker said, "you can't take it with you when you die — which you should do in about five seconds. Now, I'll ask you again . . ."

"What happened?" Felicia asked when they

came back outside.

"The Foxxes were here," Decker said, looking unhappy.

"The Foxxes?"

"That's right, the Foxxes," he said. "There's two of them, Brian and Brent."

"And they're twins?"

"Identical." He still looked unhappy.

"I told you so," Felicia said — and that was why Decker looked unhappy.

He knew she would say that.

They mounted up and headed out of town quickly.

"How long ago did they leave?" Felicia asked.

"This morning," Rebecca said. "All this riding and I miss him by a matter of hours."

"Look on the bright side," Decker said.

"Which is?"

"At least now we've got a live trail to follow."

■ ■ ■ ■

Part Three:
Foxx Trail

■ ■ ■ ■

CHAPTER XXI

Brent Foxx insisted that he felt his horse going lame and he wanted to stop in Bell's Crossing.

"We've only gone about forty miles, Brent. We've still got some daylight left."

"Just let me get the horse checked, Brian. We don't want it going lame out in the middle of nowhere."

"Let me take a look at it."

"When did you become an expert in horseflesh?"

"It's not wise for both of us to go into town together."

"Fine, let me go in and you wait here. I'll be back real quick."

Brian frowned, but then finally agreed.

"Be back in an hour, Brent, even if you have to buy a new horse."

"I'll be back, brother," Brent said. "Count on it."

■ ■ ■ ■

Brent Foxx rode into Bell's Crossing, but instead of heading for the livery stable he headed for the bank.

He hadn't looked this bank over for that long — after all, he'd simply passed through the town recently on the way to meet his brother — but he was sure that it would be easy. He'd hold it up and meet Brian within an hour, just like he'd agreed.

He left his horse in front of the bank and went up onto the boardwalk to the front door. It was getting late and he could see through the window that the bank wasn't busy. The town was a small one, and as he checked the street, he saw that it was sparsely populated.

Perfect.

He entered the bank and stood behind the elderly woman who was standing at the only teller's cage. He waited a few moments, but she was taking so long with her transaction that he finally ran out of patience.

"Excuse me, lady," he said, pushing her aside.

"Young man!" she objected, but the force of his push staggered her and she stumbled, trying to keep her balance.

He pointed his gun at the teller and said, "Let me have the money, friend, and make it quick. I got an appointment."

The teller, a young man, froze with fear.

"Come on, jasper, I ain't got all day."

When Brent poked the gun through the bars, the barrel almost touched the young man's nose. The teller pulled a bank sack over and began filling it with money.

"Where's the manager?" Brent asked.

"H-He's in the o-o-office."

"Good," Brent said, just as the office door opened and the manager stepped out.

"What the hell —" he said, staring. He was a barrel-chested man with a full mustache that hid his mouth.

"We're being robbed, Mr. Levi," the teller said, still filling the sack.

"Look here, fella —" the manager began, but the teller stopped him.

"Mr. Levi, don't you recognize this fella?"

"I do not."

"He's Brian Foxx." The teller looked at Brent and pushed the sack under the cage. "You are Brian Foxx, aren't you?"

"That I am, sonny," Brent said, accepting the sack. "Now don't anybody make a move until I'm to hell and gone, hear? I'd hate to have to shoot somebody. Understand?"

"Yes, sir," the teller said.

The manager harumphed his disapproval but remained silent.

Brent backed his way to the door, then averted his eyes in order to open it.

At that point the elderly woman, who had since righted herself, reached into her cloth bag and pulled out a small derringer.

"Mrs. Maxwell!" the teller shouted.

Brent turned in time to see her point the gun at him and pull the trigger, a look of pure glee on her face.

Gonna get me a bank robber, she was thinking.

It was her last thought in life.

Brent felt the bullet strike him in the side, like a bee sting, and fired in return. His slug struck Mrs. Maxwell in the chest and the frail woman was thrown to the floor.

"Damn you!" the manager shouted.

Mr. Levi had no gun, but Brent didn't stop to notice that. He was hurt, and he wanted to hurt back!

He fired at Mr. Levi and his bullet bisected the bank manager's mustache, taking out most of the back of his head. The teller screamed and held up his hands. Brent's next shot went right through the palm of the young man's left hand, which saved his life. The bullet was deflected just enough, and although it gave the young man a new, albeit bloody, part in his hair, the wound was not serious.

Brent opened the door and bounded out of the bank in time to see a man with a badge coming toward him.

"Hey, you —" the lawman managed to call out before Brent shot him in the chest.

Damn, the deputy thought as he was dying, first you draw your gun, then you yell, hey . . .

Brent mounted his horse, which had shown no signs of being lame, and rode hellbent for leather out of town, leaving behind him a state of chaos that would take hours to calm. By that time, he'd be well away.

But he was bleeding.

Brian Foxx heard the horse coming before he saw it, and stood up. It was then he saw his brother riding toward him for all he was worth.

"What the hell happened?" Brian asked.

Brent tossed his brother the bank sack full of money and Brian caught it out of reflex.

"Oh, Brent —" Brian said, shaking his head.

"Can't count it now, brother," Brent said breathlessly. "Might be a posse on my tail. I, uh, had a little trouble."

"Brent —" Brian said, and it was then he

saw his brother's hand clutching his side. There was blood leaking out from between his fingers. "You're hit!"

"Not bad, but we've got to get going. It'll take them time to get up a posse."

"Brent, how many people did you shoot?"

"Brother Brian," Brent said, "I lost count."

Chapter XXII

Decker, Felicia, and Rebecca made Bell's Crossing just before noon the next day. The state of turmoil was still very much in evidence.

"Something happened here," Decker said.

"What?" Felicia asked.

"That's what I want to find out. Let's find the sheriff's office."

They found the sheriff's office, and Felicia was told to stay outside with the horses, which she bitterly resented.

Decker and Rebecca walked in and found the office crowded.

A man with a badge stood behind his desk talking to five other men. Decker listened carefully.

"Matt, you take five men and ride north. Sam, take five and go south —" And so on. It wasn't hard for Decker to figure out that he was listening to a posse being deployed.

When the men had their assignments and

began filing out, the lawman noticed Decker and Rebecca.

"Can I help you folks?"

He was in his fifties, from all appearances, and Decker didn't think he had too many more posses left in him. For one thing, his hands were showing sign of arthritis.

"Maybe you can —"

"I hope this won't take long. I got a killer to catch."

"A killer?"

The sheriff nodded.

'Fella came into town yesterday, bold as you please, and held up the bank."

"And he killed someone?"

"An old woman, the bank manager, and my fool deputy."

"An old woman?"

"Sounds funny, don't it? Well, this is even funnier. The old woman, Mrs. Maxwell, she whipped out a derringer and plugged the jasper."

"How bad was he hit?"

"Not bad enough. He did all his killin' after that."

"Sheriff, what did this fella look like? Did you have a witness?"

"Sure did — the bank teller. Fella tried to kill him, too, but missed. The teller said he was Brian Foxx. You hunting this killer?"

"I am."

"And you, miss?"

"Foxx killed my brother in Arizona. I'm looking for him."

"Well, he rode north out of town, but it got dark soon after. This is the first chance I've had to get a posse together. I don't hold out much hope of catching him, so as much as I hate bounty hunters, mister, I wish you luck."

With that the sheriff pushed past them and went outside. Decker and Rebecca followed.

"Now what happened?" Felicia asked. She hated having to be filled in last.

"One of the Foxxes was here and held up the bank," Decker said. "He killed three people, including an old woman who shot him first."

"An old woman killed him?"

"She hit him, but she didn't kill him."

"Then he's traveling hurt."

"Seems like. The question is, is he traveling alone, and which way did he go?"

"We're farther behind than we figured," Rebecca said. "We stopped for the night, but after what happened here you can bet Foxx didn't."

"That's a possibility. The sheriff said he rode north out of town. Let's see what we can find."

They mounted up and rode out of the north end of town.

Since Decker was the professional manhunter, Rebecca and Felicia left it to him to search the ground for signs.

They headed south a ways, came to an incline, and rode up until they came to a stand of brush which even the women could see had been crushed down.

"Pretty clear now what happened," Decker said.

"Want to explain it to us less fortunate people who don't have your insight?" Rebecca asked.

"The man who robbed the bank switched to the south after he hightailed it from town, and then he met his partner who was waiting for him here."

"They didn't want to be seen together," Rebecca said.

"Or," Felicia said, "one didn't know what the other one was planning."

"Now, how do you figure that?" Rebecca asked.

"I've read everything there is to read about Brian Foxx," Felicia explained. "This job was pulled too close to the others, and it was sloppy. Foxx plans better than this.

I'd say that if we're dealing with two men, one was the planner, and he had nothing to do with this job."

"She may be right," Decker said, "much as I hate to admit it. What if one brother did all the planning and the other brother got tired of it?"

"So he decides to pull a job on his own while his brother waits up here," Rebecca said. "If that's the case, there's a very unhappy brother out there."

"I'd say two," Decker said. He was kneeling on the ground and got up to show them the bloodstains on his fingertips. "One's mad, and the other one's hurt."

"Well, they're farther ahead, but maybe they aren't traveling as fast," Rebecca said.

"Only one way to see if we can catch them," Decker said. He mounted up and said, "Let's get moving."

CHAPTER XXIII

"Sit still!"

"Then take it easy!"

Brian, still angry, was being unnecessarily rough as he tried to patch the hole in his brother's side.

"You're lucky it was a small-caliber gun."

"Who the hell would have expected an old woman to shoot me?" Brent said, shaking his head in wonder.

"You've got to suspect everyone. That's what I've always tried to tell you."

"Yeah, yeah, you're always telling me. Well, this time I told you." Brent reached over and grabbed the sack. "Let's see how much we got."

"How much you got doesn't matter," Brian said. "It was a fool play."

"I tell you what," Brent said, buttoning his shirt. "If you don't want half, you don't have to take it."

"I don't want it," Brian said, standing up.

He used water from his canteen to clean his brother's blood from his hands. He wished he could wash away the responsibility he felt as easily. He'd turned his brother into a bank robber, and now he'd come to this.

Well, he thought, maybe I made him a bank robber, but he made himself a fool. All he had to do was *listen* once in a while!

"Fine, then I'll keep it all."

Brent reached into the sack and pulled out a handful of bills.

"What the hell —"

"What's the matter?" Brian asked.

Brent was frantically pulling another handful of money out.

"That little son of a bitch!"

Brian walked over to where his brother was sitting and immediately saw what the problem was.

He started laughing.

"What the fuck are you laughing at!"

"You," Brian said. "You hold up a bank and take one in the side from a woman, and you end up with a bag of one-dollar bills."

"Son of a bitch!" Brent said, throwing the sack as far as he could.

"You're lucky if you've got five hundred dollars there. That sure as hell isn't worth getting shot for."

■ ■ ■ ■

The Foxx brothers traveled another two or three hours, but then Brian noticed a waxy look coming over Brent's face and saw that his brother's side was covered with fresh blood.

"Hold up," he said, grabbing the reins of Brent's horse.

"What is it?" Brent asked. It came out as almost a gasp.

"That bleeding's not stopping. We've got to get that bullet out."

"It's a tiny little bullet, Brian," Brent complained, but Brian knew how much discomfort and pain the "tiny little bullet" was causing his brother.

"We've got to get you to a doctor in the next town."

"What if there ain't a doctor in the next town?"

"Then we'll let a vet do it."

"Brian —"

"Don't argue with me on this, Brent. I'm not gonna haul your ass all over the country-side because you're too stubborn to have a bullet removed — even a tiny little one."

Brent shrugged and said, "You're the boss."

"Now that," Brian said, "is the biggest joke I've heard all day."

Chapter XXIV

"Where do you figure they're heading?" Rebecca asked.

"I figure that since there was trouble with the Doverville robbery they've decided to change the location of their operation," Decker said.

They were riding three abreast, with Decker in the center, Rebecca on his right, and Felicia on his left.

"Colorado?" she asked. "Kansas?"

Decker shook his head.

"I'd head farther east than that. I'd want to put as much space between myself and . . . what happened in Arizona that there wouldn't even be a hint of it in the air."

"And that goes for what happened in Bell's Crossing, too," Felicia chimed in.

"So then they'll just relocate and start over again," Rebecca said.

Decker nodded.

"We've got to stop them, Decker," she said. "I don't want what happened to my brother and those other people to happen to anyone else."

"We'll catch up with them," Decker said. "Even a small bullet has to be giving whichever one of them is hit some problems. They'll need a doctor unless one brother wants to take the bullet out of the other brother himself."

"That means they'll have to stop in a town," Rebecca said.

"Right."

"But which one?"

"We'll have to find out."

"That means *we* have to stop in every town."

"Pass through, anyway."

"But that'll put us farther behind!"

"We'll only pass through the towns that aren't out of the way. It shouldn't hold us up that much."

"Why don't I go on while you stop?"

"And when you catch up to them, what will you do?"

"I — I'll —"

"We'll ride together, Rebecca."

"Why don't you go ahead while Felicia and I stop in the towns?" Rebecca suggested.

"Again," Decker said, "what happens if you ride into a town and they're there?"

Rebecca didn't answer.

"I know you're anxious, but you've got to be patient."

"I'm not a bounty hunter. I haven't learned your kind of patience."

He wasn't sure if that had been meant as an insult or not.

"And you never will make a bounty hunter unless you learn."

"I have no intention of being a bounty hunter."

"Why? Don't you have a bounty on Foxx's head? And aren't you after it?"

"That's different."

"Is it?"

"Yes."

"I don't see how."

"You're after him for the money, and that's all."

Felicia started to speak in Decker's defense, but he waved her to silence.

"People have to eat, Rebecca, and to do that they have to work, and most people work at what they're good at."

"And you're good at hunting people down?"

"Yes."

"And killing them?"

"What makes you think I kill them?"

"Isn't that what bounty hunters do?"

"It's not what this bounty hunter does," Decker said, "and I don't think it's what most bounty hunters do."

"Haven't you ever killed a man after you caught up to him?"

"Yes."

"Because it was easier to bring him back that way? Facedown over a saddle?"

"Because he was trying to kill me — and you should be the one to judge? You're planning to kill Foxx when you catch up to him."

"It's different, I told you."

"Revenge is a nobler cause than survival?"

She turned to look at him and said, "He killed my brother!"

"That's fine. He killed your brother, so you kill him. See what that gets you."

"I don't want to talk about it anymore."

"You started the conversation."

"And now I'm ending it."

"Have it your way."

"I'm only riding with you —"

"Because you need me."

"I do not! We happen to be going in the same direction. I do not care to have my motives analyzed by you."

"Let me ask you one more question."

"What?"

141

"What did you do back in Doverville —
for a living, I mean."

"I . . . was a schoolteacher — but I can
ride and handle a gun as well as any man."

"You were a tomboy as a child, right?"

"What's wrong with being a tomboy?" Felicia asked. She just wanted to get into the
conversation.

"I don't care to pursue this any further,"
Rebecca said. "Could we ride in silence for
a while, please?"

"That's fine with me," Decker said. "I'm
not used to all this company on the trail,
and I'm getting a headache anyway."

CHAPTER XXV

The next town Brian and Brent Foxx came to was called Stillwell, and Brian decided that they'd wait and ride into town after dark.

"We want to attract as little attention as possible."

"Why don't you let me go in myself, get patched up, and then meet you here?"

Brian gave his brother a glare and said, "Because I can't trust you not to try and rob the bank before you leave."

Brent didn't have an answer to that, and a low moan escaped his lips just at that moment. Brian wondered if he was really in pain or just looking for sympathy.

After dark they rode into town at a leisurely pace, hats pulled down low over their faces.

A townsman was crossing the street and Brian stopped him.

"Can you tell me where the doctor's

office is?"

"It's down another block on the right, friend, but the doc will be asleep right now. You got an emergency?"

The man was squinting up at Brian, trying to see his face through the shadow.

"No," Brian said, "no emergency, friend. I'll just see him in the morning."

"Have a good evening," the man said, and continued on his way.

"We gonna wait until morning?" Brent asked.

"Hell, no."

They rode up to the next block and located the doctor's office. Brian helped Brent off his horse and to the front door, and then knocked firmly but quietly until a light came on inside.

"What in the blazes —" the man said, opening his door. He was gray-haired, of medium height, and in his fifties. "What the hell are you knocking on my door at this time of night for?"

Brian had thought of several explanations, but the doctor seemed so irate he decided to do it the easy way.

He drew his gun and pointed it at the doctor's nose. It was the sight of the two identical men as much as the gun that kept him silent.

"Inside, Doc," he said. "You got a patient."

The doctor lived alone, which was good. They wouldn't have to deal with a wife and children.

He led them to his examining room, where Brian instructed him to help Brent off with his shirt.

"You gonna tell me how to take the bullet out, too?" the doctor asked.

"No, you're gonna do that one all by yourself, Doc — and if I see you slip even a little, you'll be dead long before my brother is."

"Young man," the doctor said, discarding Brent's bloody shirt, "my job is saving lives, not taking them, no matter whose."

"Keep that in mind, Doc."

"My name is Petrie, Dr. Petrie."

"I don't care what your name is, just get that bullet out of my brother's side and patch him up good. We've got to get moving."

"Obviously you're on the run," Petrie said, examining Brent's wound.

"Stop talking, Doc, unless it has to do with my brother's wound."

"It was a small bullet, wasn't it?"

"Yeah," Brent said, grunting as the doctor probed and prodded.

145

"Still," Petrie said, straightening up, "after I've removed it he really shouldn't ride."

Brent looked at Brian and shook his head. "How long should he stay put?"

"Any period of time would be helpful, but I wouldn't want him to move for at least a week."

"Forget it," Brent said. "Get the bullet out and patch me up, Doc. We're leaving tonight."

"No," Brian said.

"Whataya mean, no?" Brent asked.

"We'll spend the night here."

"You can't stay here," Petrie said.

Brian raised his gun and said, "This gun says I can stay anywhere I want."

"You have a point. I'll need my instruments."

"Get them."

"And some hot water."

"Get that, too. I'll just tag along."

The doctor said to Brent, "Don't move from that table."

Brian followed the doctor to another room, where he filled a pot with water and set it to boil. When the water was hot, he picked up his instrument bag from a corner and looked expectantly at Brian.

"What?"

"I'll need that water."

"You want me to carry it?"

"You'd have to put the gun down to do that, but if you're afraid of me —"

"You're not that dumb, Doc," Brian said, holstering the gun. "If you make a move I'll scald you with this water."

"I understand."

They went back to the examining room where Brent sat slumped on the table.

"How you doing?" Brian asked.

"I feel pretty weak."

"It's natural that he would," the doctor explained. "He's lost a lot of blood. Put the water down here." Brian obeyed. "Lie down, young man, and we'll get that bullet out."

While he worked, he talked to Brent, as if trying to keep his mind off the pain.

"I've never seen such a perfect set of identical twins," he said. "Usually even the most identical ones have something to distinguish them. I can't find anything at all that would help me tell you apart."

"Ahhh," Brent said, and his head slumped to one side.

"Doc?" Brian shouted.

"Relax, your brother has passed out. It's just as well."

"He better be all right."

"He's fine," Petrie said, and then added triumphantly, "and here's the bullet!"

147

He held it up to show Brian and then dropped it into the basin. He wet a cloth with alcohol and cleansed the wound and the area, then applied a bandage.

"He can rest there for a while."

"We'll keep an eye on him."

"There's no need, really, I assure you," the doctor said. "He'll be fine, as long as he doesn't get a fever."

"We'll stay here and watch him," Brian said. "I got nowhere else to go."

The doctor sighed, pulled a straight-backed chair over, sat down, and promptly went to sleep.

Chapter XXVI

After they'd made camp, Felicia cooked dinner — she would have refused Rebecca's help even if the older woman *had* offered it — and Decker took care of the horses. When the food was ready, Rebecca accepted hers with a nod of her head and carried it away from the fire.

"Guess she's too good to eat with us tonight," Felicia said, handing Decker a plate of bacon and beans.

"She's got a lot to deal with," Decker said.

"Why are you making excuses for her?"

"She lost her brother, Felicia, and she's out here in the middle of nowhere, totally out of her element. I think deep down inside she's sorry she came."

"Why doesn't she go back, then?"

"She's committed to this now. To come this far and not go through with it would be to admit she made a mistake and wasted a lot of time. Also, she'd probably feel like she was betraying her brother's memory."

They sat and ate in silence for a while, and then Felicia said, "You like her, don't you?"

Decker didn't answer immediately, then said, "I like some things about her. Her dedication to her brother, her spunk —"

"The way she looks."

"She *is* beautiful."

"I knew it!" Felicia said, putting her plate in her lap. "If she came over and offered to sleep with you, you wouldn't turn *her* away, would you?"

Decker considered that question carefully. Maybe Felicia needed a lesson.

"As a matter of fact, I probably wouldn't," he said, "but then she's older than you are."

"And prettier. Go ahead, say it."

"Well, Felicia, when you're her age you may very well be prettier than she is, but right now I'd have to say yes, she's prettier."

"I knew it!" she said again. "I'm gonna eat over here!"

She picked up her plate and stalked away from the fire, staying within its circle of light.

As Felicia walked away, Rebecca decided to join Decker.

"I came over to apologize," she said,

hunkering down opposite him.

"About what?"

"About this evening, the argument we had."

"You're within your rights to argue."

"Maybe, but I also want to apologize for my attitude since we've met. I've judged you very badly and treated you badly, and you're only trying to help."

"That's all right," he said, "There's no need to apologize. You've gone through a lot."

"Yes, I have, but that's no excuse. Anyway, I just wanted to get that said."

She fell silent and began to concentrate on her meal.

"What did you do to Felicia?" she asked.

"Why?"

"She's glaring at you."

He looked over his shoulder, then back at Rebecca.

"Look again."

Rebecca frowned.

"She's glaring at *you.*"

Rebecca looked over, and Felicia averted her eyes.

"She's in love with you, you know," Rebecca said.

"She's looking for a story, looking to ride my coattails."

"No, she's in love with you," Rebecca insisted, "and she's probably afraid that I'll steal you away."

"She did ask me if I'd sleep with you — providing you made the offer, that is."

"And?"

"I said yes — just to teach her a lesson."

Rebecca looked down at the fire and said, "Of course." Decker thought he detected the hint of a smile — the first since they'd met.

"She's got nothing to worry about," he added.

"No."

"She's just a kid, anyway."

"No," Rebecca said, "she's a young woman. Maybe I should go over and talk to her. Would you mind?"

"No, not at all. Is that the schoolteacher in you coming out?"

Now she did smile and said, "Old habits are hard to break."

She put her plate down, got up, and walked over to where Felicia was sitting.

Now Felicia and Rebecca were sitting together and it was Decker who was left alone.

Maybe he'd go over and eat with John Henry.

■ ■ ■ ■

Later Felicia and Rebecca came back to the fire, laughing and talking, and proceeded to clean up. Decker was gratified to see both of them in a better mood than they had been in for some time.

He really didn't need the extra headache of having two grumpy women along.

"Should we set up a watch?" Rebecca asked.

"All right. Who wants the first one?"

"I'll take it," Felicia said, "and then I'll wake Rebecca."

"And I'll wake Decker."

"We'll take two-hour watches," Decker said, reclining on the ground with his head on his saddle. "Good night, ladies."

He tipped his hat over his eyes and proceeded to sleep as lightly as he had the previous nights.

Chapter XXVII

When Brent Foxx's head moved, Brian rushed over to the doctor and shook him awake.

"What?"

"He's moving!"

"That's because he's alive," the doctor said testily. He stood up, stretched, and then walked over to the man lying on the table. He put his hand on his head, then checked his eyes and held his wrist.

"No fever. I got the bullet out clean."

"Is he awake?"

"Not really. He'll probably sleep the rest of the night, and that's what you should do, too, especially if you plan to leave in the morning."

"That'll depend on my brother, Doc."

"I suppose so."

"Do you have any rope?"

"Rope? Why would you want — oh," Petrie said, realizing what the rope was for.

"Look, there's really no need for that."

"I am not in any shape to be argued with, Doc. Either I tie you up or I knock you out. The choice is yours."

Petrie nodded and said, "I'll get the rope."

After he had tied and gagged the doctor and left him in a corner of the examining room, Brian went over and looked down at his brother as he lay on the table.

To Brian's eye his brother looked pale and somehow smaller and younger. This was the first time either one of them had ever been shot, and Brian didn't mind admitting that he had been very frightened — but damn it, it was Brent's own fault, so why did he feel such guilt over it?

He put his hand on his brother's forehead and was gratified to find that it still felt cool. The doctor had done a good job, and he thought that he'd leave the man some money when they left.

If Brent didn't kill him.

He'd had no intention of falling asleep, and as he came awake with a start he looked around the room in a semi-panic before he realized where he was.

He stood up and rubbed his face, then checked on the doctor, who was still asleep.

"It's about time you woke up," Brent said from the table.

"You're awake."

"A lot longer than you. How about coming over here and helping me sit up?"

Brian went over and gently eased his brother into a sitting position.

"How do you feel?"

"Fine. Just get me on my horse and we'll be on our way."

"I don't know, Brent. Maybe we should stay here a day or two."

"Brian, we really don't know if there's a posse on our tail or not. If you want me to stay here I will, but you go on ahead."

"Oh, no. We either stay together or we go together."

"In that case, we'd better get going. Let's settle up with the doctor and move."

Brian frowned.

"I mean pay him something," Brent said. "He did a good job."

"All right," Brian said. He was relieved that he wasn't going to have to argue his brother out of killing the doctor. "Let me wake him up and untie him."

"He's asleep. The man's got a lot of guts."

"I know."

Brian went over to where the doctor was seated on the floor and shook him awake.

After he untied him, the doctor stood up and moaned.

"Stiff," he said, stretching.

"Sorry about that, Doc," Brent called out, "but my brother's the cautious type."

"I can see that. How are you feeling this morning?"

"Fine. You did a great job. Pay the man, Brian, and see if you can't buy me one of his shirts so we can get going."

"I'll get you a shirt, no charge," Petrie said, "but you really shouldn't be moving."

"Just give us some extra bandages, Doc, and we'll get out of your life," Brent said.

Petrie gathered some bandages and put them into a sack, then went into the other room.

"Brian," Brent said a moment later, buttoning the shirt the doctor had gotten for him, "why don't you get the horses while I settle up with the doctor."

Brian frowned at his brother.

"I'm fine, Brian. The doc's not gonna try anything, are you, Doc?"

"Not after I saved your life."

"See?"

"All right. I put the horses around back last night after I tied up the doctor. I'll wait for you out there."

"You'd better tie him up again before you

157

go. Somebody'll find him soon."

Brian retied and gagged the doctor, who didn't bother resisting.

"I'll be right along," Brent said, still working on the shirt buttons. "I want to ask the doctor a couple of things."

Brian nodded and went out the back way to get the horses ready.

Brent finished buttoning the shirt and tucked it in, wincing as he did so.

"You taped me up pretty good and tight, Doc. I appreciate that."

The doctor nodded.

"Remember what I told you about my brother being real cautious, Doc?" Brent asked, going over to the doctor's bag. "Well, sometimes he just ain't cautious enough." He took out a bottle of alcohol, looked at it, and put it back. "Sometimes," he said, finding what he wanted, "I got to be cautious enough for the both of us."

He turned away from the doctor's bag and Petrie saw the sharp instrument in his hand.

"Sorry about this, Doc," Brent said, leaning over the doctor, "but I got too much at stake, you know?"

The doctor's eyes widened as he realized what Brent was going to do, and he tried yelling to no avail. The gag was good and tight and muffled his voice, totally.

Brent grabbed the doctor by the hair and pulled his head back so that his neck was exposed. He took the knife and cut the doctor's throat in one swift, clean motion, then pulled his hand right away real quick and jumped back to avoid getting blood on the nice clean shirt he'd borrowed from the doctor.

Well, actually the doctor had sort of *willed* him the shirt.

"How much did you leave him?"

"A hundred dollars," Brent lied. "I figured that would keep him from talking."

"Good idea. Come on, I'll help you get on your horse."

Once Brent was in the saddle, Brian mounted up.

"Okay?"

"I'm fine," Brent assured him. "Hey, Brian."

"What?"

"I wanna thank you for bringing me to the doctor, even though I was stubborn about it."

"That's okay, Brent. That's what I'm here for. To take care of you."

"Yeah," Brent said. "You usually know best."

Chapter XXVIII

As they rode into Stillwell, Decker felt his instincts acting up again. The town was calm, just coming to life for the early part of the day, but he felt as if something was very wrong.

"It happened again," Decker said as they rode into Stillwell.

"What?" Felicia asked.

"Something's wrong."

Felicia and Rebecca exchanged glances and both of them shrugged. They were getting along a lot better since they'd had their talk last night, and all of a sudden they were acting like sisters. That was okay with Decker, though, because now they were talking to each other and leaving him alone.

They rode directly to the sheriff's office and Decker dismounted. In deference to Felicia, Rebecca volunteered to stay with the horses.

"Why don't you both stay with the

horses?" Decker suggested, and to his surprise they agreed.

Decker walked into the sheriff's office and decided to play it straight. The lawman was just coming out of the back room, where Decker assumed the cells were. He was of a type that Decker had seen many times before, a type that had been in the job so long that he had grown fat and satisfied. This one's belly hung over his gunbelt.

"Sheriff?"

"That's right."

"My name's Decker." Decker approached the man and took out the poster he had on Brian Foxx. He handed it to the sheriff.

"I'm looking for this man."

"Brian Foxx," the sheriff said, proving that he could read — or at least that he had recognized the drawing. "Everybody's looking for him, especially since they raised the price on his head."

"To what?"

"Twenty-five hundred. You a bounty hunter?"

"That's right."

The sheriff shrugged. It was no skin off his nose how somebody made his living. He handed the poster back.

"I haven't seen him."

"At all, or recently?"

"At all."

"If you had, would you tell me?"

"Sure, why not?" the man said, shrugging. "It's nothing to me either way."

Decker was folding the poster, wondering if his instincts had been off about there being something wrong. At that moment a man came rushing into the sheriff's office. He was out of breath and looked scared out of his wits.

"Sheriff, ya gotta come quick."

"What's the matter, Nick?"

"Ya gotta come quick!"

"Tell me what's happened, man!"

"Somebody's killed the doc."

"Shit," the sheriff said. "Oh shit." He grabbed his hat and followed the man out.

Decker walked out behind them and Rebecca said, "What's wrong?"

"I'm going to find out. I'll meet you at the saloon," he said.

He trailed along behind the sheriff and eventually found out where he was going. The shingle next to the door said, HOWARD PETRIE, M.D.

Decker walked up to the door, and since no one stopped him or questioned him, he went in. He heard the sound of voices from another room and followed them.

It appeared to be the doctor's examining

room. The sheriff was there with two other men, one of whom was the man who had run into his office. There was a fourth man there, too, but he was on the floor.

Dead.

The man had been tied up and gagged. Then his throat had been cut.

"Jesus Christ," the sheriff kept saying. "Jesus Christ . . ."

"What are we gonna do?" one of the men asked.

"Nothing like this has ever happened before," the sheriff said. "Jesus Christ."

"He was okay last night," the third man said. "I saw him in the saloon. He had a drink and then said he was turning in for the night."

Decker looked around the room and saw a bloody shirt on the floor. He moved toward the examining table and saw a basin next to it. He saw what was in the basin, picked it up, and put it in his pocket before anybody saw him.

He was taking his hand out of his pocket when the harried-looking sheriff turned around and saw him.

"Who are you?"

"Decker."

"Oh, right." The sheriff looked at the body again and then looked away. "What do I do now? Jesus Christ, I ain't never seen nothing like this."

"Well, for starters," Decker said, "you could have him taken over to the undertaker's."

"Yeah," the sheriff said, taking his hat off and running his fingers through his hair, "yeah. Nick, go and get some help. We'll take him to the undertaker's."

"Okay, Sheriff." It was the same man who had run into the sheriff's office with the news.

The sheriff looked at Decker as if he were seeing him for the first time, and asked, "What's your interest in this, Decker?"

"Nothing, Sheriff," Decker said. "I'm just passing through."

Rebecca and Felicia were waiting in front of the saloon with the horses.

"Let's mount up and get out of here," he said, grabbing John Henry's reins.

"What did you find out?" Rebecca asked.

"The town doctor is dead. His throat's been cut."

"So?" Rebecca asked.

"There was a bloody shirt on the floor."

"And?"

"What did the sheriff in Bell's Crossing say the old woman had used to shoot Foxx?"

164

"A derringer, a small-caliber derringer."

"I found this in a basin next to the doctor's examining table."

He opened his hand to show her.

A spent bullet.

A small-caliber spent bullet.

When they were clear of the town, they reined in.

"You want to explain this to us so we can understand it, too?" Rebecca asked.

"The shirt on the floor had a bullet hole which came from a small-caliber gun."

"You're saying that this is the town where one brother brought the other for treatment of his wound?"

"Right. I heard somebody say that the doctor was fine last night and that he had turned in for the night. That means that the Foxx brothers got here sometime during the night, had the wound treated, and then cut the doctor's throat so he couldn't tell anyone they were here."

"That's awful!" Felicia said. "You know, everything I read about Brian Foxx made him out to be some kind of Robin Hood, never hurting or killing anyone — and then all of a sudden people started to get hurt."

"Then my brother got killed."

"And then the old woman was shot, and

the bank manager and the deputy, and now the doctor is killed in cold blood."

"What does it all mean?"

"It means," Decker said, "that the wrong Foxx is starting to take charge, and we've got to get to them before he kills his own brother."

■ ■ ■ ■

PART FOUR:
FOXX TAIL

■ ■ ■ ■

Chapter XXIX

"What's wrong?" Brent Foxx asked Brian.

They had paused to let the horses rest — at least, that was what Brian told Brent. What he really wanted to do was allow *Brent* to rest. They were four days out of Stillwell and had just crossed into Colorado, and Brent hadn't once asked to rest. It would have been great to be able to think of the gesture as noble or courageous, but the pure fact of the matter was that Brent was too stubborn to admit he needed rest.

Now Brent saw Brian peering intently past him, back the way they had come.

"Somebody's on our tail, Brent," Brian said, squinting in an attempt to get a better look.

"Who?" Brent immediately thought of a posse from Stillwell.

"I don't know. I can't see very well, but from the amount of dust they're raising I'd say two or three riders, maybe even more."

"That's too small for a posse."

"A posse wouldn't have followed us this far from Bell's Crossing."

Brent didn't offer an opinion on that.

"What then?" he asked.

"I don't know, but we'd better get a move on if we don't want them to catch us."

"I'm ready."

"Let's go, then."

They started off again, at an increased pace.

Two hours later they stopped again and Brian looked behind them. Brent didn't turn in his saddle for fear of reopening his wound. Instead he turned his horse to face the opposite way.

"I don't see anything."

"They're still there," Brian said.

"Where?"

"Keep looking. See! See that dust?"

"I never was much good at this, Brian," Brent said, shaking his head. "I'll take your word for it that there's someone there, but what do we do about it?"

"Let's change direction," Brian said. "We'll travel south for a while, head toward New Mexico, and see if they stay on our tail."

"And if they do?"

"We'll have to shake them off."

"I know a perfect way of doing that," Brent said, touching his gun.

"We'd be outnumbered, Brent, and your hand is still a little unsteady, in case you haven't noticed."

Brent frowned and brought his hand up in front of his face where he could see it.

"I'm all right."

"That's right, you are. You managed to survive getting shot and you're all right — and I want to keep both of us that way. We'll try and shake them. That way we won't have to face them."

"Have it your way, brother," Brent said. "You always do."

But, Brent thought, things do have a way of changing.

CHAPTER XXX

"They've spotted us," Decker said.

"How can you tell?"

"I still can't see them," Felicia complained, squinting mightily.

"You can't see them, just their dust."

"How can you be sure it's them?" Rebecca asked.

"I can't, but would you rather assume that it isn't?"

"No."

"Then we'll assume that it is, and we'll also have to assume that they've seen us."

"Why?"

"They speeded up."

"You can tell that from dust?"

"This is my profession, ladies," Decker said. "I wouldn't be doing this if I wasn't good at it. They've speeded up their progress, and we'll have to speed up ours."

There were no complaints, and that was what they did. "Doesn't that beast ever get tired?" Rebecca asked, referring to John Henry.

"He never complains," Decker said. He dismounted and studied the ground for a few moments, then stood up, looking south.

"They've seen us, all right," he said. "They've changed direction."

"Where are they going now?" Felicia asked.

"I don't know where they're *going,* but they're heading toward New Mexico."

"Maybe they're not heading as far east as you thought," Rebecca said.

Decker shook his head.

"They're checking to see if we're really following them."

"And when they find out that we are?" Rebecca asked.

"Ah," Decker said, mounting up, "but they won't."

Without allowing either of the women to ask a question, he spurred John Henry on at a gallop, and they shrugged at each other and followed.

It became a cat-and-mouse game after that.

Decker planned to circle away from the Foxxes while trying to keep their progress in view. It might convince the Foxxes that they had lost their tail, and if they then slowed their progress he'd be able to catch up to them faster.

Still, with one of them wounded they wouldn't be able to move too much faster than they were at the moment. His other option was to simply run them down, but that might have put either Felicia or Rebecca in some danger.

He was in no hurry and decided to play it this way instead, trying to fool them into slowing down.

Maybe they were good at robbing banks and bad at reading the trail.

"What do you think?" Rebecca asked, coming up alongside of Decker. Her horse was laboring to keep up with John Henry. Meanwhile, Felicia had fallen behind, and if she fell any farther behind he'd have to slow down to allow her to catch up.

"They haven't slowed down any. I guess they're too smart for that."

"What's next?"

Decker turned and looked at Rebecca, then turned and looked at Felicia.

"Rebecca, I'm going to ride ahead and try to run them down."

"And what are we supposed to do?"

"I want you to stay with Felicia. She can't keep up well and —"

"Oh, no, Decker," Rebecca said. "You're relegating me to baby-sitting duty."

"Look, I can move faster without you, and I can also move *better* because I won't have the two of you to consider before I make a decision."

"What will happen when you catch them? There are two of them."

"Do you really think I'd be any more effective with you and Felicia along? Face it, Rebecca, having both of you along is slowing me down. Let me go ahead, run them down, and do my job. By the time you catch up, I'll have them both trussed up nice and neat."

"You hope."

"I hope," he said, nodding. "There's always the possibility that the ground could open up and swallow me. In that case, you'd be on your own. But that's not going to happen. I'm going to catch them and take them back into custody."

Rebecca turned and looked back at Felicia, and when she looked for Decker she found that he had already sprinted ahead of her.

"Okay," she said, "have it your way."

Chapter XXXI

"So?" Brent asked. He used only the one word because he was too busy trying to catch his breath to use any others. He had a stitch in his side, and he thought he might be bleeding again.

"Still coming. We're gonna have to keep moving, Brent."

"So let's move then."

Brian cast a dubious look his brother's way, then said, "All right."

"Something's wrong," Brian said sometime later.

"What?"

"I can't see them."

"Maybe we lost them."

"No, I don't think so." Brian looked from left to right as far as he could. He kept looking until he found them.

"I see what they've done."

"What?"

"They've gone wide instead of staying directly behind us. Whoever's in charge is pretty smart."

"Good, we'll give him a damn medal when he catches us."

Brian looked at his brother and asked, "Are you all right?"

"Stupid question," Brent said through his teeth. "You expect me to say no?"

"Brent —"

"Come on, let's keep moving. I'd rather bleed to death in the saddle than let some bounty hunter take me."

They moved forward, Brian wondering if it was indeed a bounty hunter. Those bastards didn't quit, especially if the money was good.

And after recent occurrences, Brian Foxx knew that the money on him was going to be *very* good.

"Now what?" Brent asked in annoyance. "You're doing me more damage than the damned trail with this stop-and-go shit. What are you looking at?"

"Some of them have slowed down. It looks like one of them has really increased his pace."

"One man?"

"Jesus," Brian said, "he's really coming

177

like a bat out of goddamned hell. He's gonna try and run us down."

"Let him. We'll take care of him and be on our way."

"We'll take care of him, all right," Brian said, "but we're going to have to find a place to make our stand."

"Well then, let's find it."

Brian Foxx knew the area pretty well, having traveled it before.

"I think I know the place, Brent. Let's go."

"It's about time. I thought we were going to put up a fuckin' welcome banner."

Less than an hour later Brian found what he was looking for, and the lone man on horseback was still coming, not even bothering to try and disguise his approach.

"What's that?"

"An abandoned church. I remembered it being here. That's where we're gonna make our stand."

"In a damned church?"

"You got any better ideas?"

"I ain't been to church in years."

"Well then," Brian said, "you're way overdue."

CHAPTER XXXII

Decker knew all along that for his plan to work the terrain was going to have to be flat and empty for miles. If there was a place for the Foxx boys to make a stand, they'd take it, and that would make his job much harder.

He kept riding, knowing that he was probably easy to spot now, but not caring. When they spotted him, they'd have to start galloping their horses as well, and the wounded Foxx brother would not be able to take that for very long.

It would have worked if it hadn't been for the damned church.

Decker spotted the large stone structure and slowed John Henry down. There was no doubt in his mind that the Foxx boys would be in there. One of them was probably up in the bell tower right now, watching him.

He decided that there was no longer any

rush to get to where he was going. The Foxx boys would be there whenever he arrived.

He reined John Henry in and sat staring at the church, which was less than a hundred fifty yards away. Already he could see by their tracks that they had gone into the church.

He had two options.

He could wait for them to come out.

Or he could go in after them.

In waiting for them to come out, it would be a question of who had the most provisions, especially water. Since he was traveling light — the women were carrying whatever stores they still had left — he certainly wouldn't be able to outlast them — but then he wouldn't have to. He'd only have to last until Rebecca and Felicia caught up.

That, however, would tell the Foxxes that all he had with him was two women, and that wouldn't do. They might then decide to try and ride *him* down, knowing that he was saddled with two women.

Waiting was out. It would only bring the women into range.

That meant going in after them.

It was a large church, and there should only be two of them. Surely he could find a way in once he got close enough.

Of course, the trick was getting close enough. A man in the bell tower with a rifle could hold off ten men, and he was only one.

He turned John Henry's head and urged him forward at a slow walk. He proceeded to walk in a wide circle around the entire church. If nothing else, it would confuse the men inside until he could figure something out.

CHAPTER XXXIII

"What the hell is he doing?" Brent shouted up to Brian, who was in the bell tower. Brent could see the man from one of the ground-floor windows.

"He's riding around in circles."

The man rode out of Brent's view, and he was trying to decide whether or not it was worth it to get up and walk to the other side of the church.

"Can you see him?" he called out.

"Yeah, I see him. Stay where you are."

"What's he doing now?"

"He's just walking his horse all the way around the church."

"What's he doing that for?"

"I don't know. Maybe he's trying to rattle us."

"Can you see anyone else?"

Brian took his eyes away from the man on the horse and looked around.

"Jesus," he said suddenly.

"What? What is it?"

"There's a whole crew of men riding toward us from the south."

"How can you tell there are so many?"

"Because they're kicking up enough dust for a dust storm, that's why."

"Why would a posse be coming from the south?"

"They wouldn't be. I don't think it's a posse."

"Then what?"

"They're coming this way from New Mexico, Brent. Who travels in large groups like that?"

"Cavalry?"

"They'd be riding in a column. These horses are all spread out."

"Indians?"

"Possible — or something even worse."

"What's worse than Indians?"

Brian looked down at his brother and said, "Comancheros."

"Jesus," Brent said.

Brian looked at the man again. He could tell that he had also seen the dust cloud. The man had a decision to make. He could ride off or ride to the church for cover, in which case he'd have to tangle with Brian and his brother.

Brian felt sure that the man would ride away.

He was wrong.

Dead wrong.

The crazy son of a bitch started riding hell-bent for leather for the church!

"He's coming in!" Brian shouted. "Brent, he's coming in!"

"Shoot the bastard!"

Brian leveled his carbine at the man and fired off a shot, but the bastard was moving too fast, and Brian never was much of a shot anyway.

"Fire again!"

Brian was about to shoot again when something occurred to him.

"If I fire, the comancheros or Indians — whatever they are — are liable to hear it and come looking."

"Well then get down here. Between the two of us we'll have to take him without any more shooting."

Fat chance of that. In fact, the son of a bitch was coming so fast Brian didn't think he could get down from the tower in time.

"Take cover, Brent! Take cover."

Chapter XXXIV

The church had big windows, and it had big doors, too, but the doors were closed and probably locked from the inside. The windows, however, were large and without glass.

His mode of entry was obvious.

When Decker saw the dust cloud, he knew trouble was heading his way, and he made his decision on the spur of the moment. He was going to have to take his chances with the men inside the church rather than the ones outside.

First he took out some extra shells for his shotgun and put them in various pockets. Then he dug his heels into John Henry, asking him for speed, and the little gelding responded. He heard the single shot fired at him from the tower, but knew after a second one didn't follow that it never would. They had seen the dust cloud, too, even clearer than he had.

He rode ol' John Henry straight as an arrow at the church and picked out his window.

The gelding knew what he had to do, and he did it.

He launched himself through the air, cleared the window easily, and Decker was inside.

As John Henry's hooves hit the floor, Decker launched himself from the saddle. He landed rolling and came to a stop next to what was left of a set of church pews. Meager cover at best, but at least it was something. He pulled his gun and waited for the commotion to subside.

John Henry's arrival had spooked the other two horses in the church and they began to make a racket.

Decker saw the red-haired man who had been holding the horses get pulled off his feet by them. He was not quick to rise, and Decker assumed that this was the wounded brother. The healthy one would have climbed into the tower.

As if to confirm his thought, the second man dropped down from the bell tower, hit the floor, and dashed for the pews at the far end of the church.

John Henry found himself a nice quiet corner and walked over to it to stand perfectly still. Somehow his actions dictated those of the other two horses, who followed his lead and did the same thing.

It was quiet and they could all hear the approach of thundering hooves.

"Foxx?"

"Yeah!"

"We've got to put this off until those riders pass by. I don't know if they're Indians or comancheros, but whichever it is they won't be friendly."

Silence.

"We can't stand them off alone."

Silence, and then one of them spoke. Decker thought it was the one from the bell tower.

"All right. Nobody moves until they've passed."

"Agreed."

The three of them sat stock-still and listened. From Decker's vantage point he was able to see out a front window. None of them had seen the approaching riders until it was too late. Decker had been intent on the church, and the men in the church on Decker.

Now they had to hope that whoever they were — they were surely some kind of scavengers — they wouldn't decide to check the church out for what was available.

Suddenly the riders were upon them, riding past the church. Decker could hardly see through the window because of the dust, but he saw enough to tell him who they were.

The worst scavengers on the plains.

Even worse than the Indians.

Comancheros.

Brian couldn't see Brent from where he was, but he was hoping that his brother wouldn't try anything foolish. They had enough trouble without attracting the passing riders.

The horsemen were riding so close that the church began to fill with dust that filtered through the windows. Brian craned his neck to see out a window, and his worst fears were realized as he saw the riders.

It seemed to take forever for the comancheros to ride past, and from the sound Decker guessed that there had to be at least forty of them.

Decker would have preferred to deal with Indians than with comancheros. Indians were at least honorable — for the most part. You could impress an Indian with courage, or intelligence, or sincerity.

A comanchero was the lowest form of life

on earth, as far as Decker was concerned. They were whites, Mexicans, Indians, the scum from every race imaginable, and they respected nothing and no one. And what they had been known to do with women . . .

Jesus, he thought, the women!

They were heading straight for Rebecca and Felicia.

"Foxx!"

No answer.

"Foxx!"

Could they have gotten out while the comancheros were riding by? No, their horses were still there.

"Foxx! Come on, one of you answer me!"

"Who are you?" a voice finally called out.

"My name is Decker. I'm a bounty hunter."

"You'll find this bounty the hardest you ever tried to collect," another voice said. It was the wounded one, lying on the floor somewhere.

"I have a proposition for you."

"A deal?" the second voice asked.

"Yes, a deal."

"What is it?" That was the first Foxx.

"I was traveling with a woman and a fourteen-year-old girl. Those comancheros are going to ride right into them. I'm sure you know what comancheros have been known to do to women."

"So? What's that to us?" the second man asked.

"Nothing. I'm telling you that I want out of here so I can go and try to help them."

The second man laughed harshly.

"You expect us to let you out of here? To let you get away after you hounded us this far?"

"If you make me stay, somebody's going to get killed, and it won't be me."

Again the second man laughed.

"There's two of us. How do you expect to get us both?"

"Maybe I won't. Maybe I'll just get one. Which one wants to go?"

"You're going, bounty hunter — and soon."

Decker decided to make his point a little stronger.

He stood up quickly and fired one barrel at the front door, which had been jammed shut with a piece of beam. The shot struck the partially rotted beam and almost exploded it into splinters, and the doors swung open. He then ducked out of sight and whistled.

What happened next must have really puzzled the Foxxes. John Henry started a ruckus, kicking and neighing, and it stampeded the other two horses right out the door, with John Henry on their tail.

"Now you've got no horses," Decker said, replacing the spent shell with a live one.

"That was stupid. You don't have a horse either," the second voice said.

"Oh, but I do. My gelding will simply wait outside for me."

"Then we'll take him — after we kill you."

Decker wondered why the other brother hadn't done more talking. From the way this one was talking, the other one *had* to be the smarter one.

He decided to take a chance that the smartest one, the one who had planned the jobs, was the real Brian.

"Brian, why is your brother doing all the talking?"

There was a moment of silence while the brothers tried to figure out how he knew which one was Brian. He hoped they wouldn't ask him to name the other one.

Brian started when he heard his name. He *knew* that the man was talking to him. Somehow this Decker had managed to figure out their whole scam and even knew which of them was which.

This was a dangerous man.

"What's your offer?" Brian called out.

191

■ ■ ■ ■

"It's simple," Decker replied. "I walk out of here clean and try to help my friends."

"And us?"

"You round up your horses and be on your way."

"And after you've helped your friends?"

"I admire your confidence," Decker said. "If I should avoid getting killed by those comancheros, I'll come right after you again."

"Jesus," the other brother said in disgust, "that's an offer?"

"Consider my chances against the comancheros."

"You seem pretty confident about your chances," Brian Foxx said.

"I've got an exaggerated opinion of my own abilities. What do you say?"

"I say forget it."

"We'll take it," Brian said.

"Shit we will!" Brent Foxx said. He stood up and started running toward Decker, his gun out.

At least he thought he was running toward Decker. After firing his shotgun, Decker had moved a few pews away. He watched now as Brent ran to where he thought Decker was, and then stopped in confusion.

Decker could have blown him in half, and that would have gotten him his reward.

Instead he said, "Don't move."

The man, all red hair and freckles — which stood out starkly against the pale skin of his face — turned his eyes and looked down both barrels of the sawed-off.

"Drop the gun."

The man's eyes flicked about for a moment, looking for a way out, and then he obeyed.

"All right, Brian," Decker called out, "I've got a new deal for you."

"What is it?"

"Your brother's life in exchange for your help."

"My help with what?"

"If my friends have managed to get themselves captured by the comancheros, I want your help in getting them out."

"You're crazy," Brent said.

Decker looked at him and said, "If you open your damn mouth again, you're a dead man."

One look at the man's face, distorted by rage and hatred, told Decker that he was the one who had done most if not all of the killings.

If his brother was smart, he'd say no deal

and let Decker blow this one away.

"What do you say, Brian?"

He gave the hidden man time to think it over and then prodded him again.

"I'm cocking the hammers on my shotgun."

Shit!

Damn it!

Brian was incensed. It would serve Brent right if he let Decker blow his damn head off. What the hell was he thinking, charging blindly like that?

For a moment — for a single, fleeting moment — he was tempted to let Decker kill him.

And then the moment passed.

"All right!" Brian Foxx said. "All right. We'll play it your way. You're holding the deck."

And it was stacked!

"Toss out your gun."

The gun came arcing out.

"Have you got another one?"

"No."

"All right, step out. If you have another gun, I'll kill you both."

Brian Foxx stepped out and Decker got a good look at him. Except for the fact that his color was good, he and his wounded brother were identical.

"What now?" Brian asked.

"Now you fellas are going to be a big help to me," Decker said, "a big help."

Chapter XXXV

Decker marched both brothers outside, and they were surprised to see John Henry standing a distance away — with both of their horses.

"Listen, you can't be serious about this," Brent Foxx said.

"Which one are you?"

"I'm Brent."

"I thought you knew," Brian said.

"I took an educated guess at which one of you was Brian, but I didn't know the other one's name — and yes, Brent, I'm serious. I brought those women out here, and if they've been taken I intend to get them back."

"You mean you really do have women out there?"

Decker nodded.

"A woman and a fourteen-year-old girl."

"Jesus," Brian said, shaking his head. Decker suddenly felt that perhaps this one

— Brian — really was a decent man.

Who robbed banks.

Brent, on the other hand, was crazy, and very probably a killer.

"Check your brother's wound," Decker said to Brian. "We don't want him bleeding to death."

Brian opened Brent's shirt, checked the wound, and buttoned him up again.

"It seems all right."

"Good. Let's get mounted up."

"You can't be serious," Brent said again. "You don't expect us to go up against who knows how many comancheros just because you lost your women?"

"No, you're right, Brent, I don't."

"That's more like —"

"I expect you to do it, or die. It's a simple choice, really. Even a dimwit like you can make it."

Brent Foxx's eyes flared and again Decker saw the hint of madness there. He wondered if Brian Foxx knew about it.

"Make the choice."

"We'll live," Brian said. "Come on, we're wasting time. Who knows what those women are going through?"

He seemed genuinely concerned.

They mounted up and rode north until they

started to smell coffee.

"Hold up," Decker said. He was riding behind the brothers.

He stood in his saddle and sniffed the air. Coffee and bacon.

"I smell bacon, too," Brian said. "Maybe your ladies made camp."

"I don't think so," Decker said. "We ran out of bacon three nights ago. Let's dismount."

They did so, and then Decker told Brian, "Tie your brother up."

"That's not necessary."

"Sure it is," Decker said. "Look at him, Foxx. The first chance he gets he's going to jump me and try to kill me. I can't afford that now."

"Brian," Brent said, "we can take him now. He won't dare fire when we're this close to the comanchero camp."

Decker looked at Brian, waiting for him to make a move. Brian looked at the noose hanging from Decker's saddle, and Decker couldn't tell if it meant something to him or not.

Maybe Brian read dime novels, though, because he grabbed a rope from his saddle and tied his brother's hands behind him.

"Don't do this!" Brent screamed.

"We're going to have to keep him quiet,"

Decker said, and Brian nodded.

He gagged his brother, then tied his legs. His brother glared at him murderously. Decker felt that any man who would slit the throat of a helplessly trussed-up man deserved worse than what he was getting right now.

"Good. Now let's go and take a look at what we're up against."

They crept as close to the camp as they could. It had been made at the bottom of a dry wash, so they were able to look down from some meager cover.

There were easily forty comancheros in camp, and they were milling about, waiting for the food to be ready. Their horses were picketed off to one side.

"See anything?" Decker asked.

"Not yet — wait. What's that over there?"

Brian pointed and Decker looked in that direction.

"The girl," Brian said.

Sure enough, it was Felicia. She had been tied hand and foot and was sitting near the campfire, where the cooking was being done. Every so often the man who was cooking — a fat Mexican — would reach over and pinch her as if he were testing her for cooking.

"Now where's Rebecca?" Decker won-

199

dered aloud.

There was some commotion at the farthest end of the camp and both men looked that way. What they saw was a crowd of men who were looking down at the ground. As they moved about, what they were looking at finally came into view.

"Oh, Jesus," Brian said.

They could see the naked ass of a man whose pants were down around his ankles. He was thrusting himself down onto someone at an increased pace, and it was obvious what was going on.

"Shit," Decker said with feeling.

When Brian Foxx spoke, Decker was surprised at his words and at the genuine feeling that was behind them.

The bank robber even put his hand on Decker's shoulder.

"We'll get them out," Foxx said. "I swear, we'll get them out."

"Yeah," Decker said, "but how?"

Chapter XXXVI

It was a strange alliance — Decker and Foxx. He had been tracking Brian Foxx for many weeks now, and at no time did he ever anticipate that he and his quarry would end up as allies.

They decided to wait until dark before they tried anything. If Rebecca was indeed the victim of the group rape that was going on, then attacking in broad daylight might bring a worse fate: death.

They returned to where they had left Brent Foxx trussed up and untied him to allow his circulation to flow again.

"We'll have to tie you up again when we go in to get the women," Brian said to his brother apologetically.

"You're siding with him?" Brent demanded.

"Only against the comancheros, and only to get the women out. We saw the woman being raped, Brent. The fourteen-year-old girl could be next."

"That's none of our business, Brian!"

"It's the business of anyone with an ounce of humanity, Brent."

"Humanity!" Brent spat. "What did they ever do for us, huh? We never had nothing, Brian, until we started taking it for ourselves — and that was your idea. Probably the last good one you ever had."

Decker sat back and watched the two brothers rage at each other. It was either something that was being very well staged for his benefit or it had been a very long time coming.

"And what was your last good idea, Brent?" Brian demanded. "Pistol-whipping some poor bank clerk? Killing that man in Doverville? Or the old woman —"

"She shot me first!"

"What about the doctor in Stillwell?" Decker asked.

"What about him?" Brian asked, frowning.

"Don't listen to him, Brian."

"What about him?" Brian asked again. "We left him tied up but unharmed. In fact, we paid him for taking care of Brent."

"Paid him?" Decker asked. "By cutting his throat while he was tied up? That's not a payment, Brian, that's a pay*off* for a man who helped you."

Brian looked at Brent.

"You stayed behind to talk to him," he said. "To *talk* to him, you said!"

"Brian —"

"You killed him? Cut his throat while his hands were tied?"

"Brian —"

"The man saved your life!"

"So what? He would have taken it if he could have. If you weren't there holding a gun on him."

"No, not that man," Brian said, shaking his head. "He saved you because he wanted to, because that's what a doctor does."

"Bullshit! He would have called for the sheriff as soon as we left and had a posse on our tail within the hour. We couldn't leave him alive, Brian, don't you see that?"

"No, Brent, I don't see that."

"You're too soft," Brent said. "You always were."

"And you're an animal, Brent," Brian said, staring at his brother as if he'd never seen him before. "A sick, rabid animal."

"And what do you do with rabid animals, brother?" Brent taunted. "You put them down. You gonna put me down . . . *brother?*"

"No, I'm, not going to do it, Brent, but somebody has to . . . before you kill someone else."

"Like you?" Decker asked.

"What?"

"How long will it be before he turns on you, Brian?"

"No, he won't," Brian said, without conviction.

"Look at him, Brian."

Brian Foxx continued to stare at the ground.

"Look at him!"

He looked.

"Look at his face, the look in his eyes. If you untied him now, do you know how he'd repay you? He'd kill you."

Brian stared at Brent, who looked as if he'd start foaming at the mouth any moment. He looked away, and then walked away.

It was a very long wait for darkness.

When darkness finally fell, it was Decker who tied Brent Foxx up again.

"You're a dead man, Decker. You hear me?"

Decker ignored him.

"You turned my brother against me. I'm going to kill you for that!"

"I didn't turn your brother against you, Brent," Decker said, looking down at him.

"You did that all by yourself."

Brian and Decker took their horses as close as they dared, and then left them to go on foot. They retraced their steps back to the vantage point they'd had earlier and looked down at the camp. It was lit by three or four separate campfires. They tried to locate the two women.

"I can't find them," Brian Foxx said.

"They've pitched a tent," Decker said, "probably for the leader. We'd better head for that."

"You think they're in there?"

"If they're not, at least we'll have him."

"This could get us both killed, you know."

"You want to back out?" Decker asked.

"And have to wait tied up with Brent? Not on your life."

Decker liked it better this way, too.

At least if he died tonight, he'd have company.

First they surveyed the entire layout.

The men were spread out, but in four or five distinct groups around four separate fires. There were two wagons in the camp, one at the far end, isolated, and one right near the tent. They were most likely filled with whatever booty they had collected along the way.

"We've got to come in from back there," Decker said, pointing to a place directly behind the tent.

"Why go down together?" Brian asked. "We'd have a better chance if we split up, in case one of us got caught."

Decker looked at Brian, his face expressionless.

"I know," Brian said, "you don't know whether or not you can trust me. All I can tell you is that I want to get those two women out of there almost as much as you do. The rest is up to you."

If they split up, Brian Foxx could very well ride back to his brother, untie him, and escape.

Somehow, though, Decker didn't think so. That was probably why he'd had Brian's gun tucked into his belt all the while. He took it out now and handed it to him.

Brian accepted it and looked at it.

"It's loaded," Decker assured him.

Brian nodded and put it in his holster without checking it.

"I'll go around this way and try to get to the tent," Decker said. "You go that way and see what they've got in that wagon." He indicated the one at the far end of the camp.

"Why that one? This one is much closer."

"If you had two wagons," Decker said,

"and one of them had explosives in it, where would you put it?"

Brian nodded, realizing what Decker meant. If the comancheros carried explosives in that second wagon, they would come in handy.

"All right, let's move," Decker said.

"Good luck," Brian Foxx said, putting his hand out.

Decker took it and said, "Yeah."

Damn, he thought. It was going to be hard turning this man in.

Chapter XXXVII

As Decker got closer to the camp, he could hear the sounds of talking and laughter. Some of it sounded drunken, and if indeed some of the men in the camp were drunk, that would be a help. He did not hear any women's voices.

He worked his way through the darkness, getting around behind the tent. His night vision helped him avoid a few chuckholes, and he hoped that Brian wouldn't step in any of them. Another thing that would work in their favor, if they were discovered, was the fact that many of the men around the campfires were looking *into* the fire. If things started jumping, their eyes would have to adjust to the darkness before they could adequately see anything.

Small points in their favor, he thought, when they were outnumbered twenty to one.

Finally he was directly behind the tent. Now all he had to do was work his way toward it. From where he was he could see the far wagon, but he couldn't make out whether or not Brian had gotten to it yet.

Behind the tent he paused and waited, hoping to give Brian enough time to get set.

Brian Foxx cursed as his heel slid into a chuckhole. Luckily he was able to shift his weight and avoid any injury. He worked his way carefully to the wagon, as thoughts similar to Decker's went through his mind. He was also thinking of his brother and what he had become. Had he seen the signs and ignored them? Could he have kept his brother from becoming a cold-blooded killer?

At least he'd be able to keep him from killing anyone else, but in order to do that he'd have to pay for his own crimes as well. Was he willing to do that? Well, if he wasn't, he'd be on his way back to Brent right now to untie him. The lives of that woman and the girl seemed very important to Brian at the moment, as if saving them would make up for the lives his brother had taken.

Finally he was directly behind the wagon, hoping that Decker was in position as well. Slowly he made his way to the wagon and climbed up into it. Being as quiet as he could, he started looking through it. He found kegs filled with whiskey, canned goods, some bolts of cloth they had probably stolen from some ranch house, and in the front of the wagon, right behind the seat, he found what he was looking for.

Three cases of dynamite.

Decker approached the back of the tent and took out the knife he had taken from his saddlebags. He listened intently and thought he could make out the sound of someone breathing evenly, as if asleep.

He punctured the back of the tent with the tip of his knife and then began to slit the material downward. Using his other hand, he spread the slit open so he could see inside, and managed to stop cutting just in time.

He was slicing the tent right above the supine form of a sleeping man, probably the leader of the comancheros. His pallet was right up against the back of the tent, and another six inches and Decker's knife would have poked him awake.

Decker withdrew the knife and drew his gun. He leaned in through the slit, raised his gun, and brought the butt down on the man's head. The man grunted, and there was a subtle change in his breathing that indicated he was no longer just asleep but unconscious.

Decker moved to his left, made a new slit all the way down to the floor, and stepped through.

There were two other pallets in the tent. Rebecca lay quietly on one, although her eyes were open. Her clothing was in tatters, doing little to hide her breasts and her thighs. On the other pallet lay Felicia. She was asleep, but the stains on her face indicated that she had cried herself into that state and was probably exhausted.

He went to Felicia first.

He put his hand over her mouth and her eyes opened. She was frightened at first, but then recognition dawned and she reached for him. She wrapped her arms around his neck and held on tightly, saying over and over, "I knew you'd come, I knew you'd come. . . ."

"Easy, take it easy," he told her, holding her. "I need your help, Felicia. Don't fall apart on me. Okay?"

She snuffled in his ear, then sat back and wiped her face with her hand.

"I won't fall apart."

"How is Rebecca?"

"Oh, my God, what they did to her," Felicia said, almost crying again. "When they brought her in here, her eyes were open,

211

but it was as if she couldn't see me."

"She's in shock. I'm going to need your help in getting her out."

Felicia nodded and said, "Okay."

At that moment the flap of the tent went up and a man walked in.

"Chico, the men want to know — hey, what the hell!"

The man drew his gun, but Decker was faster. He fired, catching the man square in the chest. The man clutched at his wound and staggered out of the tent.

"That does it!" Decker said aloud.

Don't fail me now, Foxx!

When Brian Foxx heard the shot, he was ready. He had tucked sticks of dynamite in every one of his pockets and in his belt. He knew that if a stray bullet hit him, there wouldn't be enough of him left to blow in the wind, but he wanted to be sure he had enough.

He was crouched down next to the wagon, watching the tent. He saw Decker go in and knew what was going to happen next, so he was ready.

As the camp came to life, many of the men looking over at the tent where the wounded man was staggering, Brian lit the fuse on the stick of dynamite and threw it.

He'd had an anxious moment when he didn't find any matches on him, but rummaging around in the wagon had produced a whole carton of lucifer-stick matches.

He threw the dynamite as far as he could, and even if it hadn't had a fuse, it would have gone off because it landed in the nearest campfire.

It exploded and two men were blown off their feet.

After that, things got pretty confused.

With the sound of the first explosion, Decker moved. He lifted Rebecca in his arms, but she didn't stir, just continued staring. He handed his gun to Felicia, and now he said, "All right, Felicia, you first. Let's go."

She nodded, stepped through the slit he'd made, and shot the first man she saw.

Once he threw the first stick of dynamite, Brian had to make a quick decision. Should he run *away* from the camp or *through* it, tossing sticks of dynamite.

He voted for a third course of action. He decided to run around the periphery of the camp, staying out of the light thrown by the campfires, chucking sticks of dynamite as fast as he could.

The comancheros were so confused that they drew their guns but didn't know what to shoot at. They had no idea how many men were attacking them or where they were.

Three or four of them, however, had more self-possession than the others.

They ran toward the tent.

As they came out of the back of the tent, a man came running around it. Felicia pointed the gun and fired, catching him right in the face.

"Good girl!" Decker shouted, not truly realizing that a fourteen-year-old girl had just killed a man!

"Move!" he told her, because she had frozen there, looking down at the man.

They started running and from behind him Decker could hear shots being fired at them. He hoped Felicia wouldn't get brave and turn to fire back.

Suddenly he felt a searing pain in his side and knew he'd been hit. He staggered from the bullet, then from Rebecca's weight, and fell. Felicia heard him and turned.

"Decker!"

Sitting on the ground, he shouted, "The gun!"

She ran to him and gave it to him. He

turned in time to see a large man bearing down on him with a gun. He fired, and the man spun and fell. There was another man right behind him, and Decker shot him, too.

There were three more men running toward him as his vision blurred, but they suddenly seemed to jump into the air and didn't move when they came down.

"Come on," somebody said, grabbing his arm and pulling him to his feet.

It was Brian Foxx.

"Take Rebecca."

"Let her walk," Foxx said. He pulled her to her feet and slapped her in the face. "If you want to live," he shouted into her face, "run!"

Felicia came forward and grabbed Rebecca's hand.

"Run!" she shouted.

Decker's legs didn't feel very strong, and as he tried to move he felt as if he were running in molasses.

"Go," he told Foxx. "Get out of here."

Brian took a stick of dynamite out of his belt, lit it, and threw it, then did the same with his last stick.

"That's it. We've got to get out of here."

"Get going!" Decker shouted at him.

"Not without you."

He put Decker's left arm around his shoulder and said, "*Now* let's go."

XXXVIII

Decker didn't know where he was.

He didn't know what day it was.

He opened his eyes and looked up and saw Felicia looking down at him.

"Oh, Decker. You're alive!"

He frowned. The statement seemed silly to him. She wouldn't have been talking to him if he weren't alive.

"What happened?" he said. "Where are we?"

"We're in an abandoned church," she said. "Foxx brought us here after you rescued us."

"When was that?"

"Two nights ago."

"Jesus," he said. "Help me up."

"You can't —"

"Help me sit up," he snapped at her.

She reached for his arm and pulled him until he was sitting. There was a dull ache in his side, and when he touched it he found that he was all wrapped up with bandages.

"Where is Rebecca?"

"She's outside."

"And Brian?"

"He's outside, talking to her. They've been talking ever since we got here."

"Tell me again how we got here."

"After you rescued us, Brian took us to where the horses were. He put you on one horse and me and Rebecca on the other and took us away from there."

He looked around the church, recognizing it as the same one where he had first encountered the Foxx brothers.

"Where's Brent Foxx?"

She didn't answer.

"Felicia, where's Brent?"

"Brian's outside," she repeated. "I'll get him."

"Felicia —" he called out, but she kept going.

He realized that he was lying on a pew bench and swung his legs off it and to the floor. The dull ache in his right side became a sharp pain, causing him to catch his breath.

"Are you all right?" Brian asked as he came up to Decker.

"Hurts like a son of a bitch!" he said through his teeth.

"I guess so. You were lucky, though. The bullet went right through."

"You doctor me up?"

Brian nodded.

"I watched when the doctor in Stillwell wrapped Brent up. I got the bleeding to stop and bandaged you. Is it too tight for you?"

"I can't tell," Decker said honestly. "It hurts too much."

"You should be okay in a few days."

"We can't stay here. We need supplies."

"We have some."

"From where?"

"I went back to the comanchero camp and did a little scavenging. I found enough to keep us going for a day or two more, if we ration it right."

"What about the comancheros?"

"Well, we killed a few, and the others scattered, I guess. They never knew what hit them, so they didn't know where to look for us. I guess they decided to cut and run."

"The wagons —" Decker began. If they had a wagon, they could get started right away.

"I thought of that, but they took them with them."

"All right," Decker said, "now where's Brent?"

Brian looked away.

"You let him go, didn't you?"

"You only need one of us to collect your bounty, Decker."

"To hell with the bounty. He's a mad-dog killer and you let him go."

"When it came right down to it, he was my brother. I couldn't let him be executed."

"I don't understand —"

"You don't have a brother. Even Rebecca understood, Decker."

"Rebecca? How is she?"

"She came around. She went through a terrible ordeal, but she's tough."

"How did you keep her from killing you?"

"She knows I didn't kill her brother."

"How did she react when you let him go?"

"She was still in shock when I did that. It was the first night."

"You let him go in the dark?"

"Yes."

"With a horse?"

"Yes."

"With a gun?"

"No . . . but he could have gone to the comanchero camp and picked one up. They were all over the place."

"He's going to try and kill us, Brian."

"He'll run."

Decker grimaced and said, "You don't believe that. He's going to try and kill us, and he'll probably save you for last."

"He's my brother —"

"Not anymore."

Decker put both hands on the seat on either side of him and pushed. He rose to his feet and felt his legs shake, but they held.

"We'd better get started."

"You can't ride."

"Your brother managed to ride with a bullet in him, didn't he?"

"A small-caliber bullet — and your wound is worse. The bullet went in *and* out. You've got two wounds that could start bleeding."

"You've got me wrapped up pretty tight. Let's take a chance."

"And where do you want to go?"

"I don't know," Decker said. "We'll head back toward Arizona and take Rebecca home."

"To Arizona?"

Decker nodded.

"I don't think she wants to go. In fact, I know she doesn't."

"Where does she want to go, then?"

"I don't think she knows. She's still pretty shook up. I think she'll just ride with you wherever you go."

"All right."

"Were you going to turn me in in Arizona?"

"If I was going to turn you in, it would be for something that you did."

"In Wyoming."

Decker looked at Brian and said, "Why didn't you leave, Brian? Why didn't you just mount up and leave?"

"You would have died, and that would have left the girls alone."

"I don't understand you."

"Why? Because I robbed banks and trains, that means I can't have compassion? *I* never killed anyone, Decker. I never even hurt anyone. I just stole from them. Believe me, they survived that."

"Look," Decker said, "come back with me and I'll stand up for you. I'll explain that there were two of you, and that the violent crimes were committed by your brother. I'll tell them what you did here for the girls, and for me."

"And then what? They'll only put me in prison for twenty years?"

"Maybe not at all. You may get a clean slate, Brian. If you do, it would be up to you what you did with it."

While Brian thought about it, Decker tested his legs by walking around. Now that he was on his feet, he was starting to feel stronger.

"Well?" he asked, looking at Brian.

"All right. I'll go back with you."

"Good. Let's get the girls and get started. How many horses do we have?"

"Four. I managed to round up some of the comanchero ponies."

"John Henry?"

"Your gelding? He's fine. Felicia's been looking after him."

"Why don't you go out and tell the girls we'll be leaving."

"All right. We'll pack up and come and get you when we're ready."

"Fine."

Brian left and Decker walked over to a window. Looking out, he thought, Brent is out there somewhere, and his mind isn't all there.

Suddenly he felt as if a Foxx was hunting *him.*

■ ■ ■ ■

PART FIVE:
FOXX TRIAL

■ ■ ■ ■

Chapter XXXIX

To Decker's complete surprise, their trip back to Heartless, Wyoming, was uneventful. He had expected Brent Foxx to try and kill them, but that had not happened.

The trial of Brian Foxx had gone as well as could be expected. Decker testified to the fact that Foxx had saved not only his life, but also the lives of Felicia Wheeler and Rebecca Kendrick.

The judge then called Decker into his chambers and questioned him about the two Foxx brothers.

"This business of twins seemed far-fetched," Judge Harold Cornwall said. The judge was an impressive-looking man, even out of his robes. Snow-white hair and eyebrows, a strong jaw, and broad shoulders added much to this impression.

"It's true, Judge."

"I know it's true, Decker. Nobody would ever concoct a lie like that. What I want to know from you is, do you have the right twin here?"

For a moment Decker felt unsure, then realized how silly the question was. This had to be Brian. For one thing, along the way they had stopped at several streams and waterholes and he had seen Brian with his shirt off. There had been no bullet wound.

"I have the right man, sir."

"And you really feel that he is worthy of a pardon for his crimes?"

Though a pardon was something you got after you were convicted, Decker knew what the judge meant, and felt it prudent not to correct the man.

"Yes, sir."

"You are acquainted with Judge Isaac Parker, aren't you?"

"I know the judge, yes sir."

Parker was known by the uncomplimentary nickname of "Hanging" Judge Parker, but Decker knew better than to put any credence in that. He had a lot of respect for Parker, a man he had met on numerous occasions.

"I asked him about you before I came here."

"Yes, sir."

"He has a high opinion of you."

"And I have a high opinion of him, sir."

"I see. Well, since the judge vouches for you, Decker, I'm inclined to put more faith in your opinion — in spite of your profession."

Fine, Decker thought, the man doesn't like bounty hunters.

"Does that mean you'll let Foxx go, sir?"

"I'll give my decision in the courtroom, Decker. That's all for now."

Decker had gone out to the courtroom and waited with everyone else for the judge to come in. When he did, he spoke the words both Decker and Foxx were hoping for.

Foxx would not be prosecuted for his crimes, as his preservation of three lives far outweighed his crimes, all of which were nonviolent.

"As for the wanted posters on Brian Foxx, they will be amended to read 'Brent Foxx,' who will continue to be wanted for the heinous crimes that he has committed."

Decker had told the judge — and testified — that Brent Foxx had escaped while he and Brian were rescuing the girls from the comancheros.

It just seemed simpler that way.

Now that the trial was over, Decker was having dinner with Brian Foxx, Rebecca, and Felicia. He was saying good-bye to all three.

"It doesn't seem fair to you," Felicia said to him.

"What doesn't?"

"Well, you brought in Brian Foxx, but you didn't get the bounty."

"They decided that I brought in the wrong man and wasn't entitled to the bounty." He looked at Brian and said, "They were right."

"Will you go looking for Brent now?" Brian asked.

"Right now I've got another poster in my pocket that I don't think will be as difficult to cash in on. As far as I know, the guy doesn't have any brothers."

"Giving up on Brent, then?" Rebecca asked.

He looked at Rebecca who, since the incident with the comancheros, seemed to have lost some of her lustrous beauty. Oh, she was still lovely, but the spark was gone, and he thought that a shame. Maybe it would come back someday. He hoped it would.

"No, not giving up," he said, "but I've got to live and I need money. I'll get back to Brent eventually. Besides, there's no telling where he's gone."

Decker looked at Brian, who looked away.

The brothers had been headed somewhere, and Decker thought that Brian had a hunch where his brother was, but he wasn't saying.

That was his right.

"What about you, Brian?" Decker asked. "Now that you're clear, you going to start all over again?"

"No, I guess I'll just start riding and keep riding until something occurs to me."

It had been Decker's experience that anyone who has ever gotten something for nothing tends to be spoiled for any kind of real job. He hated to think it, but after a few months — or weeks — of real work, he figured banks would start looking good to Brian Foxx again.

"Rebecca?"

Rebecca just shrugged and said, "I don't know. I can't seem to think straight."

"It'll take time."

"I've got a lot of that."

They finished dinner, and then Brian Foxx offered to walk Rebecca to her hotel.

"Those two make an odd pair."

"I think they make a nice couple," Felicia said.

"They make an odd couple. A few months back she was ready to kill him on sight."

"Not him, Brent."

"Yeah," he said thoughtfully, "Brent."

231

"Are you going to leave tomorrow, Decker?"

"Yes."

"I guess I haven't grown up enough for you to take me with you."

He studied her, all cleaned up and wearing a dress and looking pretty as a newborn fawn. He also remembered a night when she killed a man.

"You've grown up a lot, Felicia, but your grandfather needs you."

"I know. He lost weight while I was gone."

"I'll be back through here eventually."

"Sure you will, Decker." She stood up and said, "Thanks for dinner. I'll say good-bye now, though, instead of in the morning."

"I'll be leaving pretty early."

She nodded, leaned over, and kissed his cheek. She started for the door, then stopped and came back. The hotel dining room was crowded, but she didn't care. She put her arms around Decker's neck and squeezed him tight.

"You better come back, Decker," she said into his ear forcefully. "You better!"

She released him and ran from the room.

Decker could still feel the pressure of her arms around his neck, and decided that she was right.

He'd better.

■ ■ ■ ■

The next morning Decker checked out of his hotel and went over to the livery to claim John Henry. On the way he saw Brian and Rebecca walking down the street, arm in arm. It was not especially early, but he assumed that they were going to breakfast.

Together.

An odd couple, he thought. Nobody could convince him otherwise.

Chapter XXXX

New Orleans was different from most of the towns Decker had ever been in. He'd been to some big ones, too. San Francisco, Denver; he even went to Chicago once. None of them seemed to have the same . . . feel as New Orleans. There were large, opulent hotels, casinos, and plenty of pretty, refined women. The food, too, was different. Decker's taste buds were not accustomed to the spicy Cajun dishes that he encountered, and he took to drinking lots of cold beer with his meals.

He was in New Orleans because of a message that had finally caught up to him in Texas — which, of course, made it easy for him to respond quickly.

The message said:

DECKER,

NEED YOU IN NEW ORLEANS. WE HAVE FOUND BRENT FOXX. PLEASE HURRY. STAYING AT THE CRAWFORD HOTEL.

It was signed: Rebecca.

That surprised him. Apparently Rebecca had finally straightened out her thinking and she'd decided to keep looking for Brent.

And there was something about her message that didn't click with him. She said "we" had found Brent.

Who, he wondered, was we?

Decker arrived in New Orleans a full week after reading the message. It had been sent almost two weeks before that, and it had been two months since he had last seen Rebecca Kendrick in Heartless.

He had been so uncomfortable upon his initial arrival in New Orleans that he went looking for and found a particular hotel, though he'd never been to Louisiana before.

He knew there had to be a New Orleans House. Just being in a hotel that called itself the "something House" made him feel a little better. It showed that in some ways, New Orleans was like any other town.

After checking in, he left John Henry at the hotel livery and hired a cab to take him to the Crawford Hotel. When he arrived, he found a much more expensive hotel than he was staying in.

How was Rebecca affording this?

He went up to the front desk, where a

prissy, tight-faced clerk gave him the twice-over — twice! — and found nothing to approve of.

The feeling was mutual.

"Yes?"

"I'd like to see Miss Rebecca Kendrick."

"Is she registered here?"

"No, she's registered at the New Orleans House; that's why I'm looking for her here, friend." He leaned forward so that his face was inches from Prissy Face. "Aren't you supposed to look it up and tell *me* that?"

"Yes," Prissy Face said, "of course." He checked the register, then closed it and said with great satisfaction, "We do not have a Miss Rebecca Kendrick registered here."

"You don't?"

"No, sir."

Had he taken so long to get here, he wondered, that she had given up and left.

"Has she ever been registered?"

The man heaved a sigh, compressed his prissy lips, and checked the book again.

"No, sir. Never."

Odd.

"Thank you."

"Of course . . . sir."

He turned to leave and then a thought hit him. He turned and tried it out on the clerk.

"What about the name Foxx?"

"What about it?"

"Anyone registered here by that name?" Decker snarled. He tried to resist the temptation to grab Prissy Face by the front of his jacket and pull him across the desk.

Looking put-upon, the clerk took out the register and checked.

"Yes, of course," he said. "Foxx?"

"Foxx."

"Yes, here it is," the man said. "Foxx."

"Mister?"

The clerk gave Decker a pitying look and said, "Mister and *Mrs.*"

"Of course," Decker said.

He was having lunch in the Crawford Hotel dining room when they came in. They spotted him, waved, and hurried over.

"Hello, Decker," Rebecca said.

"Decker," Brian Foxx said.

"I hope you don't mind," Decker said, "but I told them to bill this to your room."

"No, of course not," Brian said. "That's fine."

"You two can obviously afford it."

"We have to explain —" Rebecca began.

"Sit down," Decker said. When they sat he asked, "What's this Mr. and Mrs. business?"

"That's for real, Decker," Brian said. "We

got married almost two months ago."

"In Heartless?"

"Right after we left there."

Decker mentally shrugged. People fall in love. It happens.

"And then what happened — after you turned your brother in, I mean?"

"What?" Brian said. "I haven't turned Brent in."

"Then where did you get the money for a hotel like this?"

He looked at Rebecca, who looked away almost in embarrassment.

"We have to explain," Brian said.

"Please do."

"After you left Heartless, we talked and decided that we should track Brent down."

"You had a quick change of heart, didn't you, Brian?" Decker said. "First you let him go, and then you decided to capture him."

"I didn't want to capture him."

"What, then?"

"Brent had a lot of the money we stole hidden away. I wanted him to tell me where it was."

"You never mentioned that."

"It didn't seem . . . important."

No, of course not. Even decent men are tempted by large sums of money. Brian Foxx was a prime example of that — in more ways than one.

"How did you track him here?"

"This is where we were headed when you caught up to us. We just headed this way, hoping to find him either here or along the way."

"And you found him?"

"Yes — here."

"And sent for me?"

"Asked you to come," Rebecca said.

"All right, you asked me to come. Why?"

"We want you to . . . approach him."

"Why me?"

Brian looked at Rebecca, who nodded.

"I think you were right about something, Decker."

"What?"

"I think if Brent saw me he'd kill me."

"What's your excuse?" Decker asked Rebecca.

"If I see him, I might kill him without giving him a chance to tell us."

Decker studied them both in silence. They seemed to have prospered, and in Rebecca's case she had regained her beauty. Her eyes were glowing, her hair was lustrous, and she was wearing a low-cut dress that showed her firm breasts off well.

And they were both trying to pull something on him.

"I don't appreciate being brought all this way to have the wool pulled over my eyes," he said tightly.

"We're not —" Rebecca said.

"Let me," Brian said, silencing her. "Decker, we want you to capture Brent and get the bounty."

"And you think he'll tell me where the money is?" Decker's tone was incredulous.

"No," Brian said. "That's not it at all. I think that after I let him go he went and got the money and came here with it. I don't know where he's got it hidden, though."

"And?"

"We want you to find out."

"By asking him?"

"By whatever means you have to use," Brian said.

"Wait a minute. Are you telling me that if I decide to beat it out of him or torture him, you'd go along with it? This is your brother we're talking about."

"No, not my brother," Brian said. "We're talking about my wife here. I've got a wife and I want to provide for her. It's time I stopped trying to save my brother."

Decker studied Brian's face and decided that he was serious. He was a fool, but he was serious. Suddenly the man was being controlled by a woman — his wife — to the point where he would turn in his own brother.

"What's in it for me?" Decker asked.

"We told you. The bounty."

"Uh-uh," Decker said. "Not enough."

"What do you want?"

"I want a cut."

Brian's eyes narrowed and he looked at Rebecca.

"How much?" she asked.

"Not knowing how much there is," Decker said, "I'll take half."

"Half?" Brian asked.

"Half for me and half for you."

Rebecca shook her head.

"No. A third. Brian and I will have our own shares." Brian looked at her, but then just nodded and said to Decker, "That's right. A third."

"You got a deal," Decker said. "Now all you have to tell me is two things."

"What?"

"Where is he?"

Brian frowned.

"He's in the bayou."

Decker had never been to New Orleans, but he had heard of the Louisiana bayou.

"Oh, that's fine. I've got to go in the *swamp* and get him?"

"That's what you do, isn't it?" Rebecca

asked. "Hunt men?"

"When the price is right."

"A third of what he's got hidden plus the bounty — that sounds right," Rebecca said.

Decker pushed his plate away and reached for his mug of cold beer.

"All right," he said after a healthy swallow. "The other question is for my own curiosity."

"What?"

"How do you have enough money to come to New Orleans and afford a hotel like this?"

Brian looked at Rebecca again, and she nodded. He shrugged and said sort of sheepishly, "We robbed banks along the way."

Chapter XXXXI

Decker agreed because he wanted to close the book on this Foxx-twins thing. He still didn't think that Brian and Rebecca were telling him the whole truth.

He did believe, however, that they had robbed banks in order to get the money they needed to come here. It hadn't taken Brian Foxx nearly as long to get back to work as he had projected, and Rebecca Foxx just wasn't the same person she was before she was raped by the comancheros. That incident, once she had recovered from it, seemed to have brought out a new toughness in her — that and the murder of her brother, who had been killed by her brother-*in-law*, Decker reminded himself.

Something definitely was not right here.

"We know approximately where he is," Brian said the next morning at Decker's hotel. "About two to three miles straight in, there's an island. He's there."

"An island?"

"Well, technically it's an island. The water around it isn't even knee-deep. You'll have to leave your horse at one point and walk, though. It gets pretty dense and then opens up again as you approach the island."

"How do you know he's there?"

"Well . . . I did talk to him, Decker. He wouldn't give me any of the money."

"And he let you walk out?"

"We're brothers, Decker."

"Then why are you afraid to go back in?"

"There's such a thing as pushing your luck."

Decker knew all about that.

He decided to leave John Henry behind and rent a horse. He didn't want to have to leave the gelding alone in the swamp.

Brian and Rebecca saw him off from his hotel, and said they'd meet him back at theirs later that day.

"Shouldn't take you more than a day," Brian said.

"You've got a lot of confidence in me, Brian."

"Always," Brian said, smiling.

Decker headed for the livery to rent a horse.

■ ■ ■ ■

The island was exactly where they had said it was, and by the time Decker got there his feet were soaked. On the island he removed his boots, dumped the brackish swamp water out of them, and put them back on over his wet socks. He wondered how much money Brent Foxx was sitting on. Enough, he hoped, to make this discomfort worth it.

He found the shack about a hundred yards in. The front door was hanging by one hinge and it looked deserted. He circled it first, but he didn't spot any movement inside. He looked around outside, but the result was the same. It didn't look as if anyone had been there for weeks.

He approached the shack cautiously, his hand on his gun, but he needn't have bothered. No one challenged him as he got to the door, and when he stuck his head inside, the smell hit him and he knew he wouldn't need his gun.

Brent was inside on the floor. His head was caved in, and the blood had long since caked. Maggots and flies inhabited the body, which meant it had been there quite a long time. Decker bent over and lifted Brent's shirt gingerly to look underneath.

He nodded at what he saw, and then stood up and searched the shack. He found nothing. There was, however, an empty leather satchel on the floor.

He went back outside and looked around again. Behind the house there was a tepid stream running off from the bayou. It wasn't good for anything, being too filthy to drink or bathe in, yet in one place there was a pair of boot prints indelibly set in the mud, as if Brent had squatted there every day.

Why?

Decker went over, squatted in the footprints, and stuck his hand in the water. The stream was about six inches deep, and at the bottom he felt something smooth and metallic. He reached in with both hands and found that a metal box had been buried at the bottom of the stream. He lifted it out and carried it to the shack.

Inside he forced the box open. Inside, wrapped well in pieces of a rain slicker that had been cut to size, were stacks of money. He opened one and found it dry. He opened them all and laid them on a wooden table.

They were bank notes, held together in packs by paper rings from an assortment of banks. From the looks of it, he judged there to be close to sixty thousand dollars. There was also a little something extra inside the box, also wrapped and kept dry. He put everything inside the leather satchel and started back.

His third would come to twenty thousand, plus the twenty-five hundred on Brent's head.

Not bad for a day's work.

"I'd like to see Mr. and Mrs. Foxx," Decker said to the clerk. It was the same prissy-faced man, and Decker had not taken the time to change after he had left the bayou. He had the satchel with him, and he wanted to get their business over with so he could leave New Orleans.

"Sir," Prissy Face said. Then he looked at the register and said, "Oh, they checked out, sir."

"Checked out? When?"

"This morning."

Either before or after he had left. But why check out? Why call him all this way to find a dead body and sixty thousand dollars, and then check out?

"All right, thank you."

To the delight of the clerk he left, and once outside he hailed a cab and told the unhappy driver to take him to the New Orleans House.

If he hadn't been so damned puzzled —

and tired — he might have figured it out.

When he opened the door to his room, the first thing he saw was Rebecca on his bed, naked. When she saw him, she rose to her knees and preened for him, thrusting out her beautiful breasts and sucking in her already flat stomach.

She was a vision, and he froze . . . long enough for Brian to step out from behind the door and put the barrel of his gun in Decker's ear.

"I knew you wouldn't be able to resist a pretty . . . face."

Across the room Rebecca was already off the bed and dressing, her face crimson.

"The money, Decker," Brian said. He took the satchel from Decker's hand and tossed it on the bed. Rebecca turned and opened it. Meanwhile, Brian took Decker's gun from his holster.

"I knew I could count on you, Decker."

"You killed your own brother, didn't you, Brent?" Decker asked. "I told him, I warned him that you would."

"Shut up."

"He found you on that island, where he went to talk to you, and you killed him."

"He wanted the money, all of it, he said. He walked in there like he thought he could still control me. Well, I showed him who was in control."

Rebecca had some of the money on the bed, pawing through it, and now she looked up, puzzled, as if parts of their conversation had gotten through to her, but not all of it.

"What?" she said.

"Your husband is not your husband, Mrs. Foxx," Decker said "He's your brother-in-law."

"No, it can't be . . ." she said, letting it trail off.

"Oh, I have a hunch that it is," Decker replied.

"You're saying that this is . . . Brent?" she said. "The man who killed my brother?"

"Brian went into the bayou, Rebecca, but Brent came out. You mean you haven't noticed anything different about him since then?" Decker didn't wait for her reply.

"Why did you let her send for me, Brent?" Decker asked.

"She insisted, and I didn't want to resist too much. Apparently Brian really didn't want to kill me. He thought he could talk me out of the money, the fool. I came out of the bayou and told her that 'Brent' wouldn't give me the money. I was going to sneak back in eventually and get it, but she insisted on sending for you, so I figured I'd let you bring the money out, then I'd take the two of you back and leave you with my brother. It would look like you had finally tracked him down and everyone had died in a shoot-out." He looked at Rebecca, who was just staring at him, and said, "Come on, put the money back in the bag, sweetheart." Then to Decker he said, "Besides, I owe you, Decker, don't I?"

"But . . ." she said, staring at him with loathing, "we made love . . ."

"And you were pretty good, too. Given time, I could have taught you a few things, but we don't have any more time. Put the money back in the bag and close it. We're all going for a little ride."

"To the bayou?" Decker asked.

"How did you guess?"

Rebecca picked up some of the money and thrust it into the bag, then picked up another pack and did the same. Decker watched her carefully, and this time her hand didn't come right out.

"Come on, come on, get it done!" Brent snapped.

And she did.

Her hand came out with the little "something extra" that had been in there, a .32-caliber revolver. She fired at the same time that he did, and Decker moved, throwing himself to the floor. He rolled and, groping, found his sawed-off.

He turned as Brent, bleeding from a wound on his left shoulder, pointed his gun at him.

Decker pulled both triggers and smeared Brent Foxx all over the walls.

EPILOGUE

The following day, after having settled everything with the New Orleans police, Decker packed his saddlebags. Both Brian and Brent were dead, and so was Rebecca. All the Foxxes were dead.

He put thirty thousand in one saddlebag and thirty in the other. Luckily the packs were still marked with the names and locations of the banks, so it would be easy to return the money. It never occurred to him to keep it. He made his living on bounties and rewards, and he was sure that the banks would offer him ten percent of what he returned.

That meant about six thousand dollars, along with the twenty-five hundred on Brent's head.

He wondered if there was any paper out on Brian and Rebecca yet.

The employees of Thorndike Press hope you have enjoyed this Large Print book. All our Thorndike, Wheeler, and Kennebec Large Print titles are designed for easy reading, and all our books are made to last. Other Thorndike Press Large Print books are available at your library, through selected bookstores, or directly from us.

For information about titles, please call:
(800) 223-1244

or visit our Web site at:
http://gale.cengage.com/thorndike

To share your comments, please write:
Publisher
Thorndike Press
295 Kennedy Memorial Drive
Waterville, ME 04901